Choice, Set Free
Book 1

Quest
of the
Tae'anaryn

By Dr Joseph Ireland, PhD.
"Dr Joe"

Originally Published by Wombat Books in 2014 as "The Tae'anaryn"

Copyright © Dr Joe Ireland, 2014 www.drjoe.id.au

1st edition 2013 ISBN: 9781921632327

2nd edition 2014 ISBN: 9781921632969

3rd edition 2015 ISBN: 9781518865060

4th edition 2018 ISBN: 9781728986364

5th edition 2018 ISBN: 9780992329488

6th edition 2024 ISBN: 9780645899900 in colour

Cover art by Emily Ireland 2018, Kialessa on Daz3D by Dr Joe

National Library of Australia Cataloguing-in-Publication entry Author: Ireland, Joe.

Title: Choice, set free: Quest of the Tae'anaryn / Dr Joe Ireland "Dr Joe".

Edition: Sixth

Target Audience: Primary school age. "Middle fiction".

Subjects: Individuality--Juvenile fiction. Detective and mystery stories.

Dewey Number: A823.4   F IRE

Lexile Number: 750

Pages   252

About the author

Hi, I'm Dr Joe: philosopher, educator, storyteller.

I am a science education specialist, based in Brisbane, Australia, which means I go about trying to get children (and teachers) to understand how to create knowledge through science. I have a lifelong passion for philosophy (particularly epistemology) science (as a social phenomenon) and fantasy, having written award winning fantasy for the Living Greyhawk campaign setting. I enjoy spending time with my wife and family, attending church, and in challenging people in what they think and in what they think about what they think. I also play flute.

The Tae'anaryn is a thinking book – designed to challenge readers young and old to consider the world they live in. Fantasy novels are a great way to teach, allowing us to explore worlds beyond our reach, to meet people beyond imagining and to take a piece of that experience with us when we return to everyday life. That is what I hope this book will do for you. I hope it will take you on a journey to meet ideas and individuals you might never have the opportunity to meet in any other way. Learn more, discuss, disagree, converse. I hope you enjoy *The Tae'anaryn*.

Sincerely,

Dr Joe Ireland

More wonderful titles by Creating Science & Dr Joe:

Choice, set free

Delightful high fantasy for the thoughtful young reader

1: The Quest of the Tae'anaryn

2: The Tae'anaryn and the Wizard's Apprentice

3: The Tae'anaryn and the Paladin's Squire

4: The Tae'anaryn and the Enchantress's Chrysalis

5: The Tae'anaryn and the Spear of the Troll Prince

6: The Tae'anaryn and the Khozmoh Djinn

7: The Tae'anaryn and the Voyage of Imagination's Dawn

8: The Tae'anaryn and the Crown of the High King

Engaging science fiction adventure with real science!

Space Chase 1: Arrendrallendriania

Space Chase 2: Elizabeth

Space Chase 3: Daniel

Space Chase 4: The Mechanizer

Space Chase 5: Moiya

Space Chase 6: Pancake

Dragon Riders of Pearl

Because Dragons…

Dragon Riders of Pearl 2: Seven Worlds

Dragon Riders of Pearl 3: Return of the Plague

Dragon Riders of Pearl 4: Rage of the Dragonmen

Dragon Riders of Pearl 5: Twilight of the Giants

Trilling young adult science fantasy adventure.

The world's best D&D campaigns – The Wolf in the Sky, Balor's Blade, Quill Versus the Lost Academy of Angelfall, and Hidden city of the Exiles

And don't forget – Creating Science, hands on science experiments and activities for everyone!

  By Dr Joseph Ireland "Dr Joe"

Dedicated to:

To my wife. I love her, I love her and I love her.

To my God. He's cool. To my kids. They rock.
And to you. You know who you are …

20-91-5-9   1-8   12-7   32-4-3-32-2-8-6

Contents

Table of figures

Choice, set free:
Quest of the Tae'anaryn

by Dr Joseph Ireland
"Dr Joe"

Characters and Pronunciation

Tae'anaryn: TAY – ah – NAR – rin (plural Tae'anaryl.) A race of creatures that have a human as one parent and a demon as the other. They are typically shunned by all others due to their appearance. They often gravitate to a life of crime due to the challenges of their upbringing and, arguably, the evil inherent in their nature. (from Academiclees' *The Races of Mya*.)

Kialessa: KEE-ah-LESS-ah. Main character in the story.

Kiel: KEE-el. Kialessa's almost adopted brother.

Piex: PEE-ex. Half-dragon genius; wizard.

Darrix: DAR-ix. Popular boy in college, a prayerful warrior.

Allastassia: AL-ah-STASS-ee-ah. Part dryad enchanter.

Posk: POH-sk. Half-troll untrained warrior.

Captain: The individual in charge of the king's security and army.

Priestess (or priest): A personal attendant of the king, responsible for counselling him on religious matters in the kingdom.

Steward: The one who manages the day-to-day affairs of the kingdom, directly under the king. An extremely influential individual.

Wizard (Wizardess): An individual who uses the science of wizardry to protect and counsel the king and kingdom.

Glossary

Alumium	A fantasy metal, theoretically related to aluminium
Aplomb	With skill
Commiserated	With sympathy
Copious	A lot
Derogatory	Rude, insulting
Ensaged	To express an educated opinion
Enspelled	To enchant someone or something with magic
Gawking	Looking, staring
Halcyon	Silence, or a kind of bird
Heraldry	Study of history, genealogy, nobility and their symbols
Legitimate	Legal, or true
Ludicrous	Crazy, ridiculous
Missionaries	Teachers of a particular religion who travel about trying to share their beliefs
Myriad	A countless or great number of things
Ostentatious	Overdone, proud, gaudy
Opulent	Ostentatious and expensive
Portmanteau	A word made up of two words, like 'chillax' or 'twingled'
Pantheon	A group of gods, usually belonging to a particular culture. In this story the seven major gods of this culture are usually referred to as 'the

  By Dr Joseph Ireland "Dr Joe"

	pantheon'
Saporous	Full of scent and flavour
Scribe	Someone skilled in writing, often tasked with keeping records or bearing messages for the king
Sigil	Symbol
Tedious	Boring
Tome	A big, fat book
Twingled	Portmanteau made of up twinkled and tingled
Ruing	Regretting
Walloped	To hit thoroughly
Waned	To get lazy or slack. We also say the moon is waning when it is getting smaller each night.

The Tournid Prophecy:

In days of peace this trial will come,
From lands unexpected, at the hand of but one.
Murder and mayhem to those who aren't violent,
A tyrant is born to those who stayed silent.

For evil will prosper when nothing is done,
Raising your hand to cover the sun,
Turn a blind eye to the deeds of the cruel,
Till no longer men, but demons, will rule.

Then faith must be placed in the most unlikely of kin,
And suspicion and doubt those who claim to no sin.
Though a mountain to move, by your hand it is done,
For if not by your hand, then truly, by none.

The sword of a troll king, a dragon mage beast,
Song of the sorcerer, heart of the priest.
Then friend will be foe, and foe trusted be,
To be saved only, by those who stay free.

　　By Dr Joseph Ireland "Dr Joe"

A wise king once told me that there was no one of unimportance; only those that choose to be insignificant ... but that always left me wondering what it took to make one's life one of substance? Does destiny choose the able, the blessed or the rich? Or was everything you became merely a reflection of the choices you made, and of the questions you had to ask?

– Anon, cited in 'Recollections of the Tae'anaryl'

Kialessa turned the burning coal in her hands, letting it die from the lack of heat between her fingers. The crowded tavern was silent now, two dozen tough and crude patrons brought to silence by the sight of a little girl holding a fire. Kialessa hated these moments, but she held her head up high. She did not like to let others see her cry.

'Mighty precious daughter you got there,' the man said, his voiced laced with sarcasm. It was he who had insisted on meeting her, the little girl that did not burn, as soon as he'd stopped here at her mother's inn for the night.

'Oh come on, apprentice wizards learn a trick just as impressive,' the woman he was with disagreed.

'Perhaps, but they still have skin that burns,' he argued with a dismissive wave of his hand.

Kialessa had not seen him here before, and he seemed to command a lot of respect. His skin was light, but he had slick black hair and a slender, daring moustache. He was tall and thin. He did not look strong enough to be one of the hunters or trappers that often stopped here. Kialessa thought that they looked like pirates or thieves. They probably all were, living out in the forest between the docks and the king's castle. She hated the tavern in the evenings; it was always smoky and crowded and, no matter how hard she tried, she could never ignore the faint smell of ale mixed with vomit.

He reached out then, as if to touch the tiny horns that adorned the top of her forehead from just underneath her mess of straight dark hair. She hissed at him, her burgundy forked tongue lashing out from between her pointed teeth. It brought a thunder of laughter from the guests. It always did.

He pulled his hand back as fast as a man could.

'Oh please don't, Jerik!' the woman he was with joked, making light of Kialessa's obvious discomfort, 'Can't you see she's just a little girl?'

'Yeah, but little girls grow up,' he said with a mischievous grin.

'Don't be disgusting!' the woman laughed, giving him a playful slap on the arm.

He sat back in his chair, rudely whacking both his feet up on the table with a thud. 'So, what's she good for?' he asked while all the other patrons listened in silence. 'She got any more tricks?'

But Kialessa did not want to show off any of her other "tricks".

'Now good gentles,' her human mother said in her uneducated tone as she held her by the shoulders. 'This me daughter, Kia. She be the jewel of me eye. Never was there a better daughter in all lands, and she's me saviour in the kitchen too. Make 'er hold the roast to sears it I do, nothing like hand cooked meats, eh!'

And the patrons laughed.

But Kialessa cringed. She hoped to the heavens that her mother would not make her take off her dress and show them *that* trick again. She looked up at the older woman in alarm, shaking her head. Kialessa had realised at an early age that her mother was a harsh and unkind woman; one who would usually keep her up past midnight to help out in the kitchen. She worked there with Kiel, a young boy her mother had purchased off a traveller five summers ago and whose job it was to do the dishes.

Kialessa spied Kiel then, watching from the kitchen, worry written all over his face.

I'll be all right, I can look after myself, she mouthed to him. He did not look happy. *The meat!* she ordered.

They looked out for each other, for few kind words were spoken in this inn. He was the closest thing she had to a brother, her parents having no other children. He slunk back, not a moment too soon. If her mother had seen him away from his chore, for even a moment, he was sure to meet the bad side of her good hand.

Her mother didn't look down at her while Kialessa held her breath.

'But I am sorry, gentle, that's about all there is to her,' her mother lied in an uncharacteristic show of kindness.

'Mother looking out for her little girl?' the man teased, not caring who heard. He looked around at the tavern as though looking for an old friend. 'So, she's the tae'anaryn then? Hope you don't mind me asking, who was the father?'

The mood in the inn became tense. People often asked that question, but never out loud. There were many races in the magical kingdom of Lenmer'el, but none was more feared, or distrusted, than the tae'anaryl. Everyone just assumed one of her parents was a soulless demon, which meant she was left with only half a soul. It was what the word "Tae'anaryn" meant. Most people never let her close enough to even touch them.

'I am, gentle solider!' a cheerful voice cut into Kialessa's bitter thoughts and filled the silence. It was her father, another full-blooded human, filling the mugs with amber ale at the counter. He had a large red nose that often seemed to itch and stomach too big for his belt, yet she couldn't help but smile at him. He was always looking out for her … at least, when he was sober.

'Yeah, right,' the man disagreed to the air.

''Tis true!' her father almost roared, talking him down with the sociable manner of an experienced barkeeper, keeping the whole tavern silent enough to listen. 'We're both human, I assure you. Seems she takes after her mother's ancestors, fought demons

     By Dr Joseph Ireland "Dr Joe"

in the second demon war. And the gods know none can return unscarred from those kinds of horrors.' Many patrons nodded. 'But this gem, my Kialessa, she's about all a father could ask for.' He smiled at her.

She smiled back. He was the kindest thing she knew in her world, though he was too busy with the inn, or too frightened of her mother, to have much time for her nowadays.

Her mother then carried on the conversation, chatting about the weather and local events, and after a further moment of being ignored she sent Kialessa back to her chores in the kitchen. Kialessa had just begun to relax, to think she'd escaped being treated like a circus curiosity once more, but she wasn't halfway across the room when the man yelled out again.

'Hey, what's *that*?' the man shouted, pointing at her.

She looked around in alarm in case there was something wrong, and forever wished she hadn't.

'There, look there!' he said as he pointed at the floor in front of her feet. 'She … she has a tail!'

He dashed up to her and she couldn't have dodged him if she'd tried. In a moment the cruel man swept her up from her feet and turned her upside down in full view of the tavern. She squealed, and her dress gathered around her shoulders. Then her tail – a dusk red tail the same colour as her skin, a tail that swept all the way down to her feet – was put on broad display to the gawking, hideous crowd. They erupted in laughter and pointed.

Kialessa tried to struggle in the man's hands, but he was strong. She tried to bite him, but he dodged her sharp pointed teeth, and only laughed harder. She squealed at him to put her down, but it only made the patrons laugh even more.

In her frustration and pain her eyes begun to glow red, and he stopped laughing. But the inn kept laughing and teasing. They could not see how her eyes glowed red when she was angry.

Suddenly there was a loud crack of someone striking a whip. The tavern fell silent.

It was her father.

He held the whip, and it didn't come out often. Her father was a small, sociable man in general, but whenever patrons got too violent or full of ale, her father would get out the whip.

She'd felt that whip too, once or twice.

'Put her down,' he ordered in a quiet, yet dangerous way. 'She's … missing her chores in the kitchen.'

The tavern was silent.

'Easy, gentle,' the other man whispered, a soft threat in his voice as well. 'Just having a little … fun.'

She was lowered to the ground where the man could see right into her still glowing eyes. He straightened her hair and spread out her dress, acting calm and unfazed by what he'd just seen of her.

'There you go, little one. Just a bit of fun. You didn't mind,' he seemed to almost order her to believe his words.

Her father answered for her, his voice quiet, almost like an apology. 'I hope you'll forgive me if I … disagree.'

The cruel man smiled in a forgiving, friendly manner. 'Gods know everyone has a right to disagree!' He then turned back to the silent tavern, 'Back to the drinking everybody! Who knows a good song?!' And in a moment everything in the tavern was back the way it should be, crowded and noisy once more.

Kialessa bashed through the kitchen doors with such force

they almost fell off their hinges. She saw Kiel, turning the meat with great care using the iron tongs. He looked grateful to see her. 'You all right?' he muttered, looking over at her. He always worried about her.

'Yes,' she lied, shoving him aside in her anger and shame, and then turned to adjust the coals in the bottom of the oven with her bare hands.

It was humiliating, yet for all the humiliation the cruel man's words seemed to sting at her even more. What *was* she good for? She had a tail, she had horns, and skin which didn't burn. She *looked* different. She looked like a demon, and that was how everyone treated her. They didn't seem to care how she felt, or what she thought. They always laughed or stared or ignored her.

Is this all I'll ever be? she wondered. *A circus curiosity used to entertain guests at my mother's inn? Isn't life, anybody's life, meant to mean something more?*

She turned the coals.

Is there more to life, and how will I ever find it?

She did not let other people see her cry, but silent tears of salt water cooled the coals in the bottom of the kitchen fire.

The Threat

Change, any change, is hard to bear. Sometimes we welcome change, sometimes we resist it, and sometimes it takes a near disaster for us to realise only years later that the change we've always wanted would not come without a price; at times, such a very high price …

Nemon, 3rd Sage of Lumos, keeper of times

By the next morning Kialessa had just about forgotten the whole unfortunate incident. She was down in the far paddock with Kiel, picking the late winterberries.

It was a beautiful morning, crisp and free. Kialessa loved mornings. She breathed in the fresh air, grateful to be alive. Little finches chased each other in the hedges, chatting merrily. The generous grass danced in the morning breeze like the ocean waves not so far away from her home. Somewhere deep inside that field of grass the little fairies would be playing, and sometimes she imagined she could hear them singing, and their singing would send her to sleep. And far away, beyond the mountains, mysterious dragons slumbered on mountains of treasure, or the elf queen defended her land from troll hoards. So far away …

At least she has a life, she thought. The land of Lenmer'el, her home, was a beautiful, wonderful land; a land full of mysteries she'd probably never get to explore.

But Kiel didn't see any of that. He complained out loud again as he rooted in the dirt, picking winterberries without her. With a mischievous grin, Kialessa raced up along the narrow edge of the fence, higher than a normal man. The height didn't bother her, not one little bit.

But it bothered Kiel. 'Get dooown from there!'

She laughed, and did a little skip. 'Look, I can even hop,' she told him, hopping on one leg.

'Kialessa, stop! Oh, I can't look …'

He worried a lot. It made him easier to tease. 'Hop, hop, hop!' Kialessa joked.

They were always teasing each other like this, just like a brother and sister. Their mother had told them to say he was adopted had anyone asked, but no one cared. She was always getting him into trouble and out of it again. And he always kept an eye out when they worked late into the night in the kitchen in case her mother caught her napping.

'I'm not going to fall. You've seen me do this a hundred times!' she said.

'You did fall once,' he muttered.

She smiled at him; poor worried Kiel. So she threw a winterberry at him.

It popped right on his shoulder and left a broad, purple stain. 'Kialessa!' he moaned in dismay, 'now I shall have to take a bath!'

'Whoops,' she lied, and a moment later threw another one. It splat right on his head.

'Kia –' he stumbled, lost for words. Grabbing up a huge handful of berries he flung them at her. Then he gasped with regret, no doubt afraid she might fall off.

She dodged most of them and, dancing along the edge, began flinging her winterberries at him one at a time. For a moment he just sat there, too shocked to respond. Then his face lit up with a broad grin and he began throwing berries back. He was a terrible shot, and in seconds he was covered with purple berries and she had barely a spot.

So, with a squeal of frustration, he grabbed the entire basket and lifted it over his head.

'Kiel, don't!' she tried to say, but it was too late. He swung it overhead at her …

… and missed terribly. She didn't even move. The basket whacked right into the fence near her feet and bounced off again in the direction it came, landing right upside down on his head.

For a moment there was complete silence. Then Kiel started to laugh from under the basket, and they both collapsed in gales of laughter.

'Woooah!' She almost toppled off, and they laughed even more.

Kiel pulled the basket off his head, great globs of berries clinging to his hair and clothes. Few people took a weekly bath in winter, but he'd be getting one tonight. She laughed again.

But Kiel wasn't laughing any more. Instead he looked around, turning his head this way and that as if he was trying to hear something.

She tried to get his attention once more. 'Look, I'm falling! Catch me!'

'Do you hear that?' Kiel asked, his voice filled with quiet worry.

'You look so funny …' Kialessa continued, but then slowed to a stop. The look on Kiel's face was genuine; he was really concerned. So she stopped to listen too, and almost right away she heard the noise.

It was barking. Dogs, lots of them; as if they were on a hunt. It was coming from the top of the hill, from the far side of the inn. A strange feeling settled on Kialessa, and her hands began to tingle with fear. Something about that barking made her feel nervous… very nervous.

'Do you hear dogs?' Kiel asked her.

'What do you suppose they're doing? Do you think it's a hunt or something?'

'I've got a very bad feeling about this.' Kiel was worried and, for once, Kialessa agreed.

The noise continued to grow. They'd heard dogs barking before, but this time it was different. They sounded angry. In the next moment a huge pack of dogs burst from around the inn, running at a terrible speed right towards them. Kialessa screamed in terror and the dogs barked even louder.

'Run!' Kiel shrieked, and almost fell over in the dust in his haste to flee.

Kialessa was faster. She took off across the fence without thinking, running down along the fallen edge as if it was solid ground. She didn't think to wait for Kiel. She just ran as fast as she could. Faster than she'd ever run before.

But the dogs were even faster.

She was running so hard that by the time she realised she'd forgotten Kiel she was at the bottom of the valley. She turned to call out to him, just in time to see the dogs run past him while he cringed in the grass, not even stopping to sniff him.

There were around twenty dogs, almost all from the neighbourhood. Hunting dogs and guard dogs, and they were all being led in front by an enormous greyhound. Even from this distance it fixed her in its gaze with vicious grey eyes.

This isn't happening, Kialessa thought. *They're coming for me!* She ran with all her might but she knew it was hopeless, they were so much faster. Seconds later she heard the greyhound's paws scuffling along on the ground. The next moment she felt its warm breath on her heels.

On instinct she threw herself to the soil and with a surprised yelp the dog tripped over her and crumpled to the ground. Kialessa looked desperately about for anything that could help, her heartbeat thundering in her ears. The other dogs had fallen far behind their leader, which was struggling to its feet and looking around wildly.

Then she saw a tree: a wide, sprawling pine tree. It looked very old. Kialessa had heard stories of the spirits of trees that would sometimes help travellers from the dangers of wild beasts. With all her heart Kialessa hoped this was one of those trees.

She raced up to the tree just as the dog found its feet and, pressing past a thousand twigs and pine needles, climbed as fast as she could. A moment later the greyhound was there, squeezing past the branches to snap at her feet. Yet by some miracle it never managed to grab hold of her, though it tore her dress. She dodged and weaved, kicking it in the snout and climbing even higher. In seconds, she was out of reach.

A moment later the other dogs arrived. For a moment they raced around the tree, their barking a chorus of violence. Kialessa scrambled up as high as she could. A few of them tried to climb in after her, but the branches were too far apart for creatures without hands, and little twigs and needles pricked them whenever they tried.

The greyhound stood back and watched, looking at her in the branches, while the other dogs hunted around the tree with wild, feral looks in their eyes. These were not the docile pets she'd met before. Some of them she knew; there was old Barley's beagle, and the blacksmith's hound.

Suddenly the greyhound barked what sounded like a command, and a moment later all the dogs were tearing at the bark, ripping into the tree with their teeth. They were being compelled, somehow, as if the greyhound was controlling them by evil magic. She knew that if they tore the tree down they would eat her alive.

The dogs yelped as they tore at the bark, cutting their lips and chipping their teeth. Still the greyhound drove them on. They cut a ring of bark right off, but it appeared they could not cut into the tree's trunk. It was too strong for them, and they whimpered as they continued to tear at it. At this rate, it would take them all night, and they would probably bleed to death first.

Suddenly they stopped, as if the greyhound had said

something. Slowly it began to approach the tree, its eyes boring into her soul as though they were … intelligent.

The other dogs stepped back, nursing their wounds. The old greyhound placed one paw on the trunk.

What is it about to do? she wondered.

'Go *away*!' she shouted; a voice almost too loud to be her own shooting from her throat. Her scream echoed throughout the forest and the dogs cringed at the sound. For a long moment there was silence, and the dogs looked around nervously as the echoes of her scream died in the forest.

Then the old greyhound looked up at her, its paw on the trunk, and took a breath like it was about to speak.

But before it could there was a crack like thunder at the top of the hill.

It was her father, with the whip once more. He was swaying unsteadily, already half-drunk even though it was only morning. Beside him her mother waited with a cudgel in one hand. Next to her, old man Barley stood with a branch raised like a sword.

'Flurry,' he ordered, 'off!'

Her father cracked the whip again, and suddenly all the dogs began to run away. The greyhound yelped at them as though it was barking an order, but it was no use. A moment later all the dogs fled as Kialessa's parents came running down the hill to save her. All, except the greyhound.

It raised its head and gave her a look that was difficult to understand. It seemed to be smiling, but not cruelly, as though it had nothing against her personally; as though this was all just business, or a simple misunderstanding. Then in the next moment it fled.

Kialessa could not stop shaking as her parents coaxed her from the tree. They took her back to the inn and gave her a drink softened with her father's medicine. He held her for several hours, while they discussed what had happened. Her mother railed on her like it was her fault, but her father whispered she shouldn't be out so far from the inn alone ever again. They both thanked Kiel, because he had run screaming to them, and saved her life.

***

That night Kialessa had many nightmares, but one seemed so real it was impossible to forget. She was in a dark hall made of stone. It seemed huge and richly appointed, but she couldn't make out anything in the shadows.

'You failed to bring down the tae'anaryn!' said a deep, angry voice. It was a voice that seethed with authority, power … and frustration. 'This is the first time you have **ever** failed me. How could you fail?'

'A thousand apologies,' another man whimpered in a smooth voice. She'd heard that voice before, she knew she had, but for all the world she could not remember where. Smooth voice continued, 'I fear destiny may have been against our cause this afternoon. We had her, but a tree nymph helped her. We took care of the nymph.' He laughed in a cruel manner.

'Irrelevant,' the powerful voice said. 'Do you know what I'm trying to do here? Do you know what I'm trying to achieve? If you know so much about destiny, then you know we cannot let an ignorant child stand in our way. You know what she may become …'

'A servant to our cause, one way or the other.'

'That is beside the point. She has the sign. You know it. You saw it. Nothing stands in the way of our cause more than one such as the King of Lenmer'el, and none stand between the king and his demise more than one such as *she*.'

'She has the sign, but not the calling, I can assure you,' the smooth voice replied in a relaxed drawl. 'Her eyes only know fear, her hands only the coals at the bottom of the oven.'

The other voice did not reply for a while. 'She has no idea of her potential, or what she may become?'

'None.' Smooth voice seemed to mock. 'But surely she has as much potential to become an agent to our cause as an enemy?'

The powerful voice seemed to consider this. 'Keep your eyes on her then, for now. Watch what she will become. As for you, you know what to do. Begin the negotiations.'

'And if the King of Lenmer'el opposes our suggestions?' Smooth voice questioned in such a sarcastic way it implied he didn't need information, only permission.

'Kill him,' Powerful voice replied.

It was like a knife to her heart, though she didn't know why. She woke up sobbing. Kiel was beside her, he'd had his arm around her all night, and for once she didn't push him away.

But the dream had made so little sense she put it out of her mind, forgetting all about it for many weeks, and went back to more sensible nightmares: dogs and trees and searing meat.

She'd been scared to death, chased up a tree by a pack of murderous dogs driven mad by evil magic. Most of them would have been put down by their owners by now. It was sad; they were innocent, too. Kialessa thought how she had almost died. But her uncaring mother had put her back to work again that evening, turning the baking cuts of lamb with her bare hands once more.

So this is my life, Kialessa thought to herself the next morning after the shock of the attack had just about worn off. *My mother owns a tavern, and I am one of the attractions. I guess it's all I'll ever be.*

And that was why she, and everyone else, were very surprised when the king's guard came that morning to take her away.

I often wonder if the most powerful enemy you'll ever face is not your foe, nor a dragon that has you pinned to the wall. It is not the wizard's dire enchantments, or even the voice of your own addictions. It is the call of a safe, familiar home. It is a well-meaning friend or family member who with soft words and kind deeds will try to keep you from risking everything to live your destiny. Who can stand against such adversaries to live their dream?

Darrix the Devout, from 'Advice to warriors'

A lazy dawn had just pulled itself from the sleepy horizon, fresh dew melting from the grass, when bright pennants of blue and gold came into view. Six of the king's soldiers crested the morning hill. They had steel swords and polished boots, shining helmets and flags atop their lances. Kialessa was terrified and inspired all at once.

Quick as she could she hid herself by the water barrel,

slinking down beside its weathered wood and the crumbled mortar of the inn.

Soldiers meant trouble. As soon as they turned up, mother would make sure the secret drawer under the bar was shut tight and locked, while father kept them talking. Sometimes they'd argue with mother till father would press some coins into their hands, and then they'd go away. Mother and father always lied to them when they asked about how much the inn was gathering in money, or when they asked who had stayed to drink here. Once the soldiers had lain in wait till a certain bandit lord came to drink. Kialessa wasn't allowed to see what happened, but the battle was brief before they'd captured their man and taken him to the king's court for justice. She never saw that bandit lord again.

Kiel came up beside her then, apron rustling as he approached. He'd never had any real idea how to keep quiet. 'What's going on?'

She hissed him to silence. 'King's guard.'

'What do they want?' Kiel asked, his voice tense with suspicion.

They were talking to her mother now, just a bit too far away for Kialessa to make out what they were saying even though she listened with all her might. Their leader was a tall, important looking woman with a massive broadsword at her waist.

What is the king's guard doing here this morning? Kialessa asked herself. They didn't look like they wanted a drink.

Then she heard a word that stole her breath.

'… the tae'anaryn …' she heard their leader say.

Without warning one of the soldiers turned and looked over

to where they were hidden. But instead of shouting out he tapped his leader on the shoulder and pointed to where they were.

'They've seen us!' Kialessa whispered.

'What do they want?' Kiel whispered back, peering further till their hiding place was well and truly unmasked.

'Me,' she whispered, and she covered her mouth.

Kiel looked over at her with a worried look on his face. 'Run.'

They could have chased after her, yet they would *not* have caught her even though she was a child and they were adults. She knew the land too well, and all the best hiding places.

Unfortunately their leader was far too clever, and knew a trick that meant there was no place in the world that they couldn't get her. 'Call your child,' she ordered her mother.

Her mother pursed her lips in a frustrated frown, and shouted, 'Horns! Get yer tanned hide out 'ere this instant!'

There was nowhere to escape now.

'Run!' Kiel repeated.

'I'll be all right,' Kialessa said, though she no longer believed it. Out she came, dressed in her only dress, the one she worked and slept in. The bucket was filled to the brim with water, but she carried it anyway. She looked out at the tall and polished guards, distrust written all over her face.

Her mother scowled at her as if this was all Kialessa's fault.

1 Kialessa looked out suspiciously, still carrying the bucket

The one who'd seen her first walked up to her and looked at her with a gentle smile. He bent down, till his nose was equal to Kialessa's. He studied her horns, her red tanned skin, and her hands. Not once did he laugh. Not once.

'Stay yer 'ands, gentle!' her mother ordered.

Their leader laughed. 'She seems a bit underfed.'

Her mother was angry. 'She works 'ard, but I keeps her well if that's what yer meaning. But why'd the king's good soldiers be troublin' themselves with a child this morning, in especial a tae'anaryn? Aren't there *thieves* to catch in the forest?' Her voice was rimmed with sarcasm.

'Plenty,' the sergeant replied in a dry, professional tone that indicated she was bored. 'But we have a command from the king's steward that concerns your "daughter". So why are we discussing such things out here? Has the hospitality of your inn waned of late?'

Her mother drew breath, as if to shout at the sergeant, but then her father intervened from inside.

'Come in, good gentles!' he said, opening his arms in a welcoming gesture. 'Where are our manners? Please, stay your beasts in the stable –'

'We'll not be in this dumping ground long enough to wet our throats,' their leader replied with a rude sneer. 'Not if I have my say. But we'd best discuss this indoors anyway.'

They filed inside, metal boots clomping on the hardwood floors and leaving mud trails. Two soldiers stayed outside by the beasts they rode. Once inside another two took up guard at the windows, weapons drawn. They looked tense and uneasy.

Her mother took a chair and her father poured himself a drink at the bar. Kialessa went to stand away by a pillar, well out of reach of the soldiers.

Their leader dragged in a large breath through her nostrils. 'Ugh! Smells just as putrid as ever. You know,' she said to her father, as though talking business to an old friend, 'you really ought to think about getting some new customers. The ones you have here –'

'Just tell us why yer 'ere,' her mother demanded.

After a moment of heated silence, the leader handed her a piece of paper.

Kialessa's mother pretended to read it, but she couldn't really

By Dr Joseph Ireland "Dr Joe"

read that well. In fact, she really couldn't read anything at all except the labels on the wine bottles, and she'd never bothered to teach Kialessa. 'So?' she demanded, fidgeting just a little.

' "So?" ' their leader mocked her. 'The king has accepted your daughter into his college. And you say "So?" '

For a moment her mother said nothing, her mouth dangling loose at the hinges.

Neither did Kialessa. *The king's college?* She pondered. *Isn't that only for royalty? A place of privilege, where the nobles' children go to learn? Why am I being invited to join the king's college?*

Then, without warning, her mother burst into tears. Kialessa knew they were not genuine tears for her own sorrow, but the empty tears she always cried when she wanted something from someone.

'Not me daughter, not me Kia,' she pleaded, reaching out suddenly and grabbing her, crushing Kialessa's head to her bosom. 'We needs 'er. She 'elps in the kitchen! What'll we do without 'er?'

But Kialessa was still too surprised to think. She tried to disentangle herself from her mother's crushing grip, excited thoughts rushing through her. *I will see the king! I will see the princesses! I will learn how to read!*

Their leader looked at her mother, her lip curled with disgust.

'Here,' she said, and flipped a small coin at her. It was solid gold. Usually only the nobility showed gold; them, and perhaps the bandit lords.

'Noooo,' her mother continued to wail. 'You cannot pay me for me child!' She held on to Kialessa so tight it was getting harder and harder to breathe. 'You cannot have 'er!'

'Oh **please**, it's not like you'll never see her again. She can be back for the midwinter festival, if you wish. Look, she will be cared for properly in the king's court, by the college headmistress. She'll face the greatest tutors in the land, she'll eat at the tables of the king's servants, she'll …' and the sergeant prattled on and on.

But then Kialessa felt a pang of fear. Should she really leave her parents till the midwinter festival? *That is almost a year away! Will I live at the castle without my family? And what if the other students didn't like me, or I don't understand what is going on? Will I be all right? What am I to do?*

She looked over at her father. To her surprise he was crying too, but not the same way as her mother was. His were silent tears. She watched him, and saw him turn away from them then. He turned to look out the window, out past the trees. There were mountains there, but Kialessa knew when her father looked out there he was not watching the mountains. He was seeing far beyond, out into a wide and wonderful world she knew he would never touch.

He used to tell her about that world, where knights fought dragons, and enchantresses hurled bolts of lightning. Where queens commanded armies, and daring thieves would steal the dinners of gods. He would tell her all these stories when they worked together in the kitchen, at least till she was old enough for her mother to insist she do it alone. Kialessa had always felt that something had happened in his past. Something had stopped him. Something had convinced him that the world past the mountains was just too dangerous a place for a person like him.

Their leader again sighed. 'Here,' she huffed. 'Another eight silver coins for your troubles. It should more than compensate you for your *employee*. More than enough to purchase another slave like that waif you got who does the dishes,' she teased. Slavery was illegal. *Very* illegal.

'How *dare* you!' her mother replied at her suggestion, her own tears drying in an instant. 'Me daughter is not going with such ill-bred –'

'No!' Kialessa shouted, making up her mind in that same instant and wrenching herself from her mother's arms. She recognised a chance to change her life, and wasn't going to miss it for anything! She was tired of the inn; tired of not knowing the world beyond the mountains. She was tired of being her mother's slave.

'What?' her mother, the sergeant, and her father chorused all at once.

'I'm not staying here!' Kialessa shouted at her mother for the first time she could remember. Then she calmed down. She didn't like shouting, and it seemed to only make other people shout more. 'I'm leaving with the soldiers. I want to go to the king's college; I want to learn what's in the world beyond this stupid smelly inn. I want to learn how to *read!*'

Her mother stammered, 'But … Kia …' she pleaded, probably more worried about losing another gold coin than her only legitimate child.

But her father burst out from behind the bar and ran towards her, hope beaming from his eyes as he thrust back his tears. 'Yes! Yes, Kialessa. You will go. You were meant for this!'

'What?' her mother protested, trying to hold him back.

'Keep *silent*, woman!' her father commanded. Kialessa had never heard him stand up to her mother like that. Never. 'For just this once,' he said, 'you will *not* hold her back!'

Her mother's mouth opened in surprise. Then it popped shut again. Then, with a furtive glance, her mother pocketed the coins. 'It's worse than 'ighway robbery to steal me only daughter from me …' she protested.

Their leader sighed in exasperation once more. 'May I remind you that as one of the king's people you have no say in what becomes of her now the king has spoken. It is only his magnificent benevolence that sees you holding almost half a year's employ for this child. That's equivalent to twenty silver!'

Kialessa squealed with delight and started running around in circles. Her mother had taken the coins, and that meant she was going! Her father had to reach out and grab her by her shoulders to stop her spinning into a chair.

'My little Kialessa,' he whispered, 'I knew from the first moment I held you that you were destined to do great things in this world! Go, Go! And become one of the king's finest!'

'But father … I'm only a tae'anaryn.'

'And you are my daughter –' he started to reply.

'Hrmf,' scoffed their leader with a rude laugh, gathering her gear, 'The child of thieves, who consort with demons …'

Her father glared at her, but spoke instead to Kialessa. 'You listen up. I always *knew* you were meant for something more than this … than this life you were born in to. You will do such great things, no matter what anyone says!' He bent down to hug her. Then he stood up again, clearing his throat. 'Now go,' he gruffed, 'gather your things!'

She turned to run up the steps, so excited she nearly fell over. Then she stopped. She realised that all she owned was the dress she wore, and a few pebbles she'd picked up on the road once or twice. Her bed was the straw that kept the stove. Gather her things?

She turned and asked, 'What things?'

He burst out laughing. Then, though she'd never expected it, he reached behind the counter and handed her his whip. It was a fine old leather whip: cracked, and well worn, with a dark brown handle with thin strips of plaited leather braids that tapered to a well-used tip. It was short, but noisy; just right for breaking up bar fights, or chasing away wild animals. She'd never known a day when he didn't hold the whip.

'And if any of those naughty noble boys come too near you … whack!' He pushed it into her hands.

'Oh, daddy!' She flung herself into his arms. 'But you need it here!'

'Not as much as you'll need it there!' he said. He sniffed as happy new tears snuck down his face and into his messy little beard. 'Take it, and remember that I love you and that our love will always protect you.'

'Come, child!' the sergeant ordered.

Kialessa turned and ran out the door, smiling from ear to ear. Their leader turned to speak to her parents some more Kialessa only heard the first few words they spoke.

'Are you sure she will be safe there?' her mother sniffed.

'Safer than she's ever been here,' her father muttered.

Kialessa ran out to look in awe at the six beasts the soldiers rode.

'Here, tae'anaryn!' the first soldier said, the one who'd spotted her. 'You ride with me.'

Kialessa ran up to the beast with excitement and apprehension.

It was a posk. She'd never ridden a posk before.

The soldier patted his saddled and harnessed beast with great affection. 'Riumi is one of the gentlest, but don't get her mad! Posk are fearsome opponents in a battle.'

Kialessa looked at its shaggy brown fur and broad shoulders. Its thick neck was hidden behind a massive head that sprouted two short tusks. 'I've never …' she began.

'Oh don't worry, posk are tame, especially this posk. They eat mostly grasses, which is fortunate, because their sharp teeth and claws mean they could eat almost anything if they wanted to. And see, their feet are like cats'. They have soft pads that don't tear up the ground when they run. Most of these beasts are bred to pull the farmers' ploughs, but some posks like these are bred for battle as mounts for the king's guard.'

With that, the soldier reared his beast up and, with a solid roar, it tore at the air with its claws. Kialessa leapt back in fright, but it calmed down right away at the soldier's command. Kialessa looked in its enormous deep dark eyes and, although it regarded her with animal indifference, she thought she saw kindness there.

The soldier offered her a hand. As she took it he hefted her up with such force she sailed through the air to land on the beast's back, squealing in fear and delight.

'Come, child,' the guard said in his firm, yet kind, voice. 'I am Noe-esk, and as we journey together would you like me to tell you a little about the king's college?'

'Yes please!' Kialessa said, her eyes wide with enthusiasm.

She gripped the beast's armoured saddle as tight as she could. 'Do you know about the lands beyond the mountains?'

'Yes, and much more.'

'King's guard!' The mounted leader ordered their attention. 'We ride to the king's gate!' With her free hand she took a trumpet. Breathing in deeply, she let out a loud, clarion call that startled the birds from the trees. Within its sound, Kialessa felt her old life end, and her new one begin. She was going be a student at the king's college!

Her mother wept for selfishness, her father for pride. They waved her off, her mother's hand in her apron no doubt fondling the new coins she'd earned. No doubt her tears would be stayed the moment Kialessa was out of sight.

But there was one sight that worried Kialessa as she rode away from her old life. It was the little boy who was watching out from behind the barrel of water, his washing apron wrapped around his waist. He put his face in his hands and cried as hard as she'd ever seen him cry, pressing his small human body against the cold uncaring stones of her parents' inn.

The King's College

Sometimes it all comes down to one choice. One decision. And that decision is not yours to make. Do you think that destiny will deny it to you? That you will miss out on everything just because one person stood in your way and, with the best of intentions, refused to give you what you needed because they couldn't see what you could? They cannot – unless you give up.

– From 'The year in jail', by the Tae'anaryn.

The journey was magical. They raced through the land and Kialessa was amazed at how fast posks could run! They passed by a flock of colourful loreb birds, and a stretch of walking elm trees. She saw a group of far hoppers, and even caught a fleeting glimpse of a gleaming spring wosk. She tried to tell Noe-esk, but the wind stole away her breath in the guards' rapid retreat from her old life. It wasn't even midday by the time Kialessa caught her first glance of Lenmer'el, the legendary castle that was at the centre of their kingdom. Its broad, crenulated outer wall was fastened securely to the bedrock with the help of dwarven stone-smiths over a hundred years before. The bright blue and gold banners of the king flew from every tower. She couldn't wait to start her classes!

But the college was not what she'd expected.

First, they made her take a bath. The walls of the washing room were cold and thick; expertly cut stone with no sign of the cheap mortar that held her old home together. An old washer woman supervised the bath, tutting in disbelief. Kialessa's hair was tattered and unkempt; her mother had dealt with it by cutting it almost as short as boy's hair. The washer woman proposed cutting it all off to deal with the lice. But as soon as someone told her that 'this tae'anaryn' was immune to fire she poured hot oil on and set her on fire. Hot enough to make her yelp, but to Kialessa it felt divine. Soon, she'd probably stop itching altogether.

'As for this rag …' the washer woman stated, and threw her only dress in a heap in the corner. Kialessa didn't care what happened to it. Secretly, she imagined being dressed like a princess; in a real dress with perhaps an underskirt and blouse. She held her breath as the old washer woman even got one out as if to consider giving it to her, but then she put it away. Without explanation she stepped out for a moment.

Kialessa was just beginning to relax, soaking herself in a nice warm bath that was little more than a barrel cut in half, when suddenly the door swung open and another serving maid came in with a heavy load of laundry. She took one look at Kialessa swishing in the tiny tub and turned pale.

'I'm –' Kialessa began.

'Demon!' the young serving maid screamed at the top of her lungs, dropping her laundry everywhere. Kialessa almost fell out of the bath in fright.

In the next second the guard sergeant kicked in the door and rushed in. She drew her sword and pointed it right at Kialessa, the dangerous and sharp steel a hair's breadth from her throat. 'What are you up to, *monster*!' she demanded, poised to strike at any instant.

Kialessa trembled with fear. She had never been threatened by a sword before. She couldn't move, and there was nowhere to flee. She went just as numb as when the dogs had attacked her.

'Off with you two!' the washer woman suddenly shouted as she ran back in, 'can't you see the child is just having a *bath*?'

The sergeant eyed Kialessa with murderous suspicion as she trembled. 'You're not at mummy's inn anymore,' she told her, 'better get used to the *real* world.' She stormed out, her wicked laugh echoing in the empty corridor outside.

'Never mind them,' the washer woman told Kialessa, giving her a towel to wipe away the tears as she held back unwelcome sobs and trembled in shock, but the woman was still careful not to touch her. 'Just forget it.'

Kialessa dried her tears and tried to pretend that hadn't happened. It was just a silly misunderstanding. She nodded, and tried to smile, but knew she'd never really feel safe here again.

Then the washer woman helped Kialessa out and handed her a plain blue dress, at least one size too big.

'All the students wear this,' the washer woman explained.

Kialessa didn't really believe her, but slipped into the dress anyway. At least it would keep her warm, Kialessa hated the cold.

Then the washer woman took her out past the stables, past a crowded and messy castle kitchen. Then she took her to the keeper of the children, the headmistress. She pushed past a creaky old door and into a tiny office where an old woman sat; dressed only in grey. Kialessa thought her face looked as if it hadn't smiled in a thousand years. She was sitting at an even older oak desk, glowering over a dozen pieces of parchment and paper, and beyond her lay the dozen, triple layered bunks of the girl's dormitory.

'Ahem, headmistress?' the washer woman interrupted, fidgeting with the hem of her dress.

The headmistress kept her face in the parchment for a moment more, before lowering her eyeglasses to scowl at them. 'Yes?'

'I bring you the Tae … the newest student.'

The headmistress harrumphed, and studied Kialessa. There was no kindness in those grey eyes. She looked her up and down, like a butcher considering her next purchase.

'Why's she wearing that old rag?'

The washer woman stuttered in her reply. 'It's … it's … what all the students are wearing, your honour.'

The headmistress glared her to silence, then glared again at Kialessa. When she spoke, her old voice was dark and threatening. 'You, child, will listen to every word I say and act on it immediately. If you give us any trouble, I am authorised to use this!'

With an explosive BANG, she brought down a cane on the desk.

Kialessa and the washer woman both jumped.

'I have had dealings with your kind before,' the headmistress said, forming each sound with careful and deliberate spite, 'and I assure you, if you so much as put one hoof out of line …'

Crack!

There was a moment of silence as the headmistress glared at her. Kialessa tried to stop the tears welling up in her eyes, but it was useless.

'I see we have an understanding,' she said. Then she spoke in a voice that might have almost been tender. 'You will sleep on the third bunk, bottom tier,' she ordered, pointing. 'Go. You may put your possessions there.'

Kialessa didn't move.

'Did you not hear what I just said?' the headmistress shouted, her voice angry and terse once more.

'I … I don't have any possessions,' Kialessa stammered.

The headmistress glared at her. 'What is that around your waist?'

Kialessa gasped. She'd forgotten about her father's whip. She pulled it from her waist where it was serving as a belt, and held it nervously in her hands.

The headmistress gave her a withering stare that seemed to say, *You're going to be trouble, aren't you?*

'Put it in the chest by your bed. Go child, it'll be safe there,' she said, her voice soft and kind once more.

Kialessa didn't believe that.

She walked along the rows of beds that filled the girls' dormitory. Surely they didn't all sleep here? Hers was a smelly sheet stretched out along two poles, the third underneath two other beds and so low it touched the stone floor. The other beds were founded on boards of wood and arrayed with duck feather mattresses and embroidered sheets.

Kialessa doubted her bed would be better than a pile of hay by a warm stove, and the blanket looked like some kind of thick cotton, not at all like the warm sheep skin rugs she could sometimes pull over herself. It made her feel sad to think she would have to learn how to sleep on that.

She carefully pulled back the covers. There was no pillow. Ignoring the headmistress's advice she hid her father's whip under the sheets, deep at her feet. If anyone found it, it would be gone for good, and the first place to look would be the chests at the foot of the beds. She wished with all her heart that it'd be there when she looked for it again.

'Now,' the headmistress commanded, 'come with me.'

With that, the headmistress started to talk. 'As a student at the king's college you experience a privilege less than one in a thousand children of the land enjoy. You are to begin classes at dawn and so must arise and ready yourself from first light. Lunch is at noon and dinner at dusk. You are to eat with the other servants and students in the servant's hall, then …'

But most of the rules the headmistress said made so little sense to Kialessa she soon found herself lost in a forest of words. When was bedtime? What was a curfew? How many times was she to wash her hands? How was she to address the ladies of the court? And how on earth was she to tell the servants from the ladies again? 'But …' she stammered.

'Hush, a student of the college will always know when to keep silent,' the headmistress instructed. She left Kialessa still lost in a forest of rules that continued till they reached a large oak door bound with iron bands. Then the old woman turned and bent down to examine Kialessa close up.

'Why they put you in that silly dress I'll never know,' she muttered to herself, straightening it out. She licked her thumb and rubbed it hard on Kialessa's cheek. Then she straightened out Kialessa's hair and, humming to herself, muttered out loud, 'Better see what we can do about those …'

She pulled a large burgundy scarf from her pockets and quickly tied it around Kialessa's head, holding all her hair back. It *was* pretty messy. With a satisfied huff, the old headmistress turned and knocked on the door.

'Now, child, you're not to ask any questions. If you so much as – ' she threatened Kialessa in a terrifying voice. Then the door opened.

'Good morning! Gods be with you on this wintery day!' the headmistress called in her friendliest voice possible. Kialessa jumped at the sudden change in her demeanour again. Perhaps she really was some kind of half evil, half friendly monster?

She certainly was terrifying enough.

A guard moved aside as she swept in pulling Kialessa along with her. Inside was a robed man, adorned with an expensive gold chain and wearing a huge emerald ring.

It was the steward, the chief of all the king's servants. He too, it seemed, was busy pushing papers.

'Ah, headmistress. What have we here?' he said, not glancing to look up as he scribbled with a quill on various parchments. All around the room, books, posters, maps, scrolls and pieces of slate lay in a reasonable order. Several guards stood alert around the room, and one or two scribes hustled about their business.

'I bring you the newest student to the king's college,' the

headmistress announced.

'And?' he asked, unimpressed. That was, until he looked up. 'Oh, I see. The tae'anaryn … why is she wearing that old rag for a dress?'

The headmistress was stuck for words and, when they came out, they were all weak and sorry. 'It's … what all the students are wearing nowadays, m'lord.'

The steward gave her a dubious stare.

Kialessa heard the old headmistress gulp with fear. He walked out from behind his desk and approached them both. He was *really* tall. His ears were just a little pointy. He was probably part fey; there was fairy or pixie heritage in there somewhere. Kialessa too found herself swallowing hard under his imperious glare.

'Can you curtsy?' he asked in a commanding tone.

She tried, just like her mother had taught her.

'Not so low child,' the steward instructed. 'You're not out on a farm anymore. We cannot have anyone thinking less of you now that you're here.'

'Yes, gentle, lord,' she muttered a mixed-up combination of the most formal replies she'd been taught.

The headmistress twisted her hands in apology. 'Her parents owned a tavern out on the road to the docks. You can imagine …'

But the steward waved her to silence. 'We needed more time to teach her etiquette,' he said, sighing with regret. 'The other students have already begun their studies this week. The king has asked to start her immediately.'

Then he noticed her head. 'Take off that ridiculous scarf! Only the married women go about with their heads covered.'

She did as he ordered, but saw his face turn into a deep frown once she did. Was her hair such a disgrace?

'Oh, I see …' he said, eyebrows raised. 'We'll she'll just have to bear it, I assume. After all, there's no secret she is a tae'anaryn anyway …'

That's when Kialessa finally realised what they were all worrying about. The horns.

They weren't worried about her hair; they were trying to hide her *horns*! Why did everyone have so much trouble with her horns? They weren't very big. They never got in the way and, sometimes, they were quite useful. She could hang things on them if she wanted. It shouldn't matter that she *looked* different.

She looked up at the steward, angry at him, and he glared back at her with a look of disdain.

'Be that as it may,' he continued, 'you are to begin your studies immediately. You can start with studies of the elements and alchemical lore this morning. You can read, I presume?'

She shook her head as he returned to shuffling his papers.

'Good,' he said, not even noticing she'd said no. 'But first, there is business to attend to. The oath. You see, my child, the purpose of the king's college is to bring out the best in our people, to make our kingdom a prosperous nation. But in order to be that we must all be united under the kind government of the regent. You will learn many things in these halls. Many skills, and many secrets. Before we teach them to you the people of our good kingdom must know you have their best interests at heart. And the best way to know if you have the people's interests at heart is to know that you have the king's best interests at heart, that you are willing to protect him and all his people with your life. King

Dunnkan is perhaps the greatest king Lenmer'el has seen in its entire history. So!' he said as he pulled a jewelled sceptre from his robe.

But Kialessa was a little lost in her own thoughts. King Dunnkan? She'd known about him all her life, but her parents had never spoken well of the man who claimed to need their taxes. She found herself wondering why the king would need her to make an oath to protect him. Wasn't he *the king*?

'Repeat after me,' the steward was saying, 'by my honour and the gods, I … um, sorry, what was her name again?'

'Oh, Kia, sir.' The headmistress said.

'Kia. By my honour and the gods, I Kia – '

'Kialessa,' she corrected them.

They both looked furious. She couldn't understand why no one used her real name; the name her father always used.

'Right, then.' He held out the sceptre.

It was black, but not scary. It had a polished diamond sphere in the end, with the king's mark clearly cut inside its hard surface. Inside, it glowed with magic power.

'What is that?' she whispered.

The steward held it up proudly. 'This, child, is the rod of the king. It contains great power: the promise of every citizen of Lenmer'el to protect their king and country. It has many abilities; tempering the weather, granting strength in war, *Veridictus* –'

'What's *Veridictus*?' she asked, trying not to notice how impatient his eyes were becoming.

'You'll find out one day. Too many powers to mention right now. Come, come, dear, put your hand here,' he said, but did not touch her.

Many? And no doubt that 'many' included the ability to bind citizens to their oaths.

Binding magic …

'Say: "by my honour and the gods," state your name …'

She didn't move. It wasn't that she didn't want to; it was just that she wasn't sure of making an oath to protect someone she didn't even know.

'But I don't *know* the king. I've never even met him,' Kialessa whispered. The steward, headmistress, and several of the guards sighed and shook their heads.

'No one just walks in to see the king in person,' the steward explained. His voice was patient but his teeth clenched. 'Even his body is sacrosanct. Not even nobles are allowed to touch his person. Why do you need to see the king?'

The headmistress laughed and patted her on the head, her voice too kind. 'Silly child, you're not making a very good impression, are you!'

The steward waved his hand as though to sweep away a misunderstanding. 'Look, child, it's just a simple oath to ensure that what you are taught is used in the best interests of the king and the people. You do want what's best for the people, don't you?'

Kialessa did, but she didn't know anything about the king. What kind of person was he? Did *he* have his people's best interests in mind?

'But I've never even *met* him,' she repeated, just a little louder. It was not that she was being rebellious, it was just, well, even her *mother* knew better than to take an oath she wasn't sure she could keep. Everyone honoured the king. He was, after all,

     By Dr Joseph Ireland "Dr Joe"

the king. But, how could she make an oath to protect someone with her life that she didn't even know?

Suddenly the old headmistress grabbed her by the neck of her dress. 'Listen, child …' she began, a crony finger jabbing right at Kialessa's nose. The angry monster had arisen again.

The steward rubbed his face in frustration. 'I told him this would happen! It's a *tae'anaryn*, by the Lasting's name!'

The headmistress continued to chide her. 'You won't be able to sit down for a week! You're **such** a naughty girl. How can you dishonour your parents like this. And the king! What will he say?'

They looked at her, expectation written all over their faces.

But there were some things Kialessa feared more than a spanking. Making a promise she didn't know she could keep was one of the worst things she knew she could ever do. Even with binding magic.

Especially with binding magic!

'I honestly don't *know* what he'll say,' she said, feeling bold. 'I've never even *met* him.'

Then the headmistress slapped her across the face and, in all honesty, it was one of the gentlest slaps she'd ever received. She could still stand up and everything. Oh, it made a huge noise and her cheek still stung, but she had to hide her face so that the headmistress couldn't see she was almost laughing.

And suddenly the steward burst out laughing, too. 'Fine then! To the king it is!'

Everyone in the room gasped in surprise.

'I *told* him it'd be like this!' The steward said, gathering some parchments and ordering a messenger run ahead of them. ' "A tae'anaryn" he said. "Very clever people". Harrumph. The

Tae'anaryl make all their own rules and then mumble, mumble mmm. Well, the king will just have to learn from his own mistakes once more!'

A second later they marched out of the door, four guards in tow, while the headmistress stood gaping, speechless in surprise. Kialessa heard her mutter, 'But *I've* never been to see the king …'

And Kialessa, who was left holding the burgundy scarf in one hand, took advantage of the situation and tied it around her waist.

She was going to see the king!

The King

Every now and then in life you're going to meet someone so amazing, someone who makes you believe you can be something better, someone who has such a profound effect on your life that it is changed forever. Don't forget them. Don't ever forget them!

– Anon. Cited in 'Recollections of the Tae'anaryl'

Four guards, the royal steward, and one young tae'anaryn child in an overlarge blue dress. Wherever they went, women curtsied and men bowed. Fully armed guards saluted. The steward hardly acknowledged any of them, except certain nobles, who he acknowledged by name. He moved with such purpose and speed Kialessa could hardly keep up.

'We'll go by the arena,' the steward muttered to her as she scurried along at his heels. 'Give you a chance to see some of the older students. There's a new batch every two years, you're part of the most recent.' He adjusted his ring and muttered more thoughts to himself.

At length the arched stone hallway they passed through opened out along one side to reveal a wide, grassy field.

'What luck,' the steward muttered. 'They're outside practicing for battle.'

Kialessa slowed in awe till one of the guards picked her up by her waist to keep her moving. She squealed in surprise.

Older youth swung swords, bashing each other's helmets and shields. One in a robe threw a bright incantation of sparkling lights, making his opponent fall over. Another two hefted broad padded axes while they tried to knock each other from the swinging log they rode. Many rushed to climb over a wall in some form of obstacle course. They each fought with dedication and intensity, with great skill and individual talent. Even some of the young lords and ladies, wooden daggers in hand, fended themselves in full finery from pretend assassins and thugs. There were humans, half fey and part dwarves. There were even tiny gnomes, no bigger than she, and far stranger youths from faraway lands; blithlings, terranoid. Even a cervitaur.

'Poor kids,' a guard muttered. 'Don't get out much with all that study.'

'Look at them go for it!' The other guard laughed. 'Rank amateurs!'

But to Kialessa's eyes they were full of skill.

'What else do they do?' she asked, and as she did a whistle blew. In a moment, they were all lined up like soldiers. But she didn't get to see what happened next. She was picked up once more by the soldier and was whisked along the stone corridor.

 By Dr Joseph Ireland "Dr Joe"

They were heading toward the central castle now, and the guards they passed became taller and stronger. One even had green skin and protruding canine teeth; clearly a half troll.

They passed by a wizard's study full of books and strange bottled potions, then through a beautiful, serene garden where an enchanted harp played to nobles as they rested. Towards the inner keep now, where huge stone statues of men turned their unblinking eyes to watch her. Up more stairs and by then Kialessa was quite out of breath. Then they stopped outside a massive polished wooden double door inlaid with silver.

A wizard stood there, blocking their way. He wore a midnight blue cloak with gold runes along the edges that spoke of hidden, arcane knowledge. As Kialessa watched in wonder a soft rainbow light shimmered from the dark insides of that cloak. His hat was crooked and blue, and in his hand he held a short, crooked staff topped with a glowing purple stone. He was tall, with pointy ears and dark eyes; a true elf.

'Steward,' he said, in a voice so soft you had to stop to hear it. 'You bring the tae'anaryn child?'

'She's right here,' he said in a humbled voice to the wizard who outranked him in power, but not authority.

The wizard looked down at her. She hoped he didn't turn her into a toad.

'I take it none of you bear our king ill?'

They all swore an oath, but Kialessa kept her silence.

At that, the wizard looked down at her. He seemed to peer into her soul. 'Hmmm,' was all he said after a moment. 'You may pass.'

Kialessa breathed a sigh of relief. The steward nodded.

The room they entered was unlike any she'd ever seen. It was huge, with royal paintings and ornate tapestries. The lounges were made of brass and were so well polished they would be blinding in the sunlight. The floor was set with a mosaic of stones and metal cut into the form of a stylised sun: probably protection enchantments, too. And on either side of the far doorway bronze statues of men stood holding broadswords twice her height.

It was a room fit for a king.

'Where is he?' she whispered.

The steward laughed. 'Well, he's not in this foyer that's for sure. I'd say he's over there, in the throne room.'

The guards chuckled.

They went in. It was bigger than her parents' inn! The walls were covered in beautiful tapestries that went all the way to the floor. The furniture was plush and noble, and sculptures of serene beauty decorated the walls. Somehow the room was warmed to the temperature of a comfortable spring day. At the far end was a throne of wood inlaid in pure gold.

But the king was not on his throne, he was standing by an ivory table with some other people, talking to an old lady who was smiling. His royal red robe went all the way to the floor and at his side there hung a glowing sword of pure gold.

In spite herself, Kialessa began to tremble. It really was the King of Lenmer'el. *What have I got myself into?*

The old lady saw them and pointed, smiling.

The king turned around. 'Steward!' he shouted in a deep voice that was full of friendship. 'The messenger told me you were coming.' He walked towards them.

His face was round and heralded a dignified chestnut beard,

speckled with white. His clothes were a royal red, clasped by an ornate gold buckle and thick leather belt. His eyes were bright and cheerful, and seemed so very old and wise.

'To what do I owe this unexpected visit?' the king asked.

'Forgive me, your highness, but your newest student, the one you ordered personally, refused to take the oath of loyalty till she'd met you in person.'

He laughed again. 'Well then, send her in, send her in!'

'She's right, oh …' The steward was looking around to see her, but by now Kialessa was hiding so far against his robes that he couldn't see her at all.

Finally he stepped aside and then there was nothing between Kialessa and the king.

Her hands trembled, her lip trembled. She was terrified. Frightened tears forced themselves to the corners of her eyes. The King stopped laughing.

'Oh child,' he said in a kind voice. And then, for the first time in her life, an adult knelt down on one knee so that they could talk to her face to face.

'Kialessa,' he said.

It was her name. It was not Kia. It was not 'the tae'anaryn'. It wasn't even 'Horns'. It was her name. Immediately, she stopped her sniffling.

'You are welcome here,' he said in a comforting voice.

And suddenly, without knowing why or bothering to ask if she had permission, she flung herself into his arms and burst into tears, burying her face deep into his speckled beard. The guards begun to move but he waved them aside and instead, hugged her good and well.

Slowly, the guards left the room.

Kialessa cried for quite a bit. The King didn't say anything, but let her tears roll down his beard and onto his royal clothes. He pulled from his pocket a hanky, white as linen, soft as a feather, and embroidered with the royal pennant. She wiped her tears and held him close.

'Little Kialessa,' the king said. 'Did you know I've known about you since you were born? I've watched you, through my servants, your whole life, and I know you to be a good person. I have asked you to join my college –'

'But why?' she interrupted him through her mess of thoughts and tears. 'Why me? I'm not good for anything, except cooking meat.'

'But no!' the king shook his head to disagree. 'I've known hundreds of people my whole life, and it has taught me two things. First, there is no such thing as a person of insignificance. My life has been changed by cutlery maids as well as kings. *All* people are great.'

'And what is the second thing?' she asked.

'Few people rise higher than their self-doubt.' He sighed. 'You can be born a queen, but if you don't believe you're anything more than a cutlery maid, then that is all you'll ever be.'

He held her away so that she could see into his eyes. 'Look around you, Kialessa. You're going to meet nobles from far off lands, emissaries from kingdoms too numerous to see in a lifetime, people of skill and ability. What makes them great? Yes, there's talent, but talent is not enough. There's the station of their birth. It helps, but it's not everything. What makes them great? Young princes and princesses from their earliest memories are told by their parents and everyone they see that they are destined for greatness. It's all they hear and it's all they believe, and when it comes time for them to wear a crown they do so *gladly* because they are *convinced* they are filled with greatness. Thankfully, by then they usually have become great because they work hard, listen well and learn much.'

Kialessa thought about that. He was so much like her father. Like her father *should* be. Until today, she'd never heard anyone tell her she might do great things. Until today, she was just a servant, and now she stood in the king's palace.

He continued, 'And I have lived to see princes raised as kitchen hands who became no more than that, notwithstanding who their parents were. Some will try to tell you differently, Kialessa. Some will try to tell you that what you are is inherited from your parents, your social status, or your opportunities in life. Don't believe them. Whether you become great is a choice you make, not a life you're born into.'

His words were like angels, and they felt true. But a little question formed inside her mind. 'But,' she said, 'why do you have the college?'

He smiled. 'You are clever. If anyone can become great, then why all this education? You know, I am the only king in the Great Kingdom who has such a large college, and I'll give you three very practical reasons. First, it gives everyone a chance, not just those who are born into wealth. Some of the greatest souls are born into poverty and it's a nation's loss that does not educate its poor. Second, it enriches the people. A few well-educated individuals will change a nation, given time. And third – I'll not hide this truth from you, Kialessa. It helps limit my number of enemies.'

'Enemies?' She knew kings had enemies, but who could possibly be this man's enemy?

'Indeed. By training the most talented students of my people it is my hope, thus far not in vain, that they will show me appreciation and perhaps even be willing to protect my people, and me. A king has many enemies, Kialessa, and not all of them are of this world.'

Kialessa looked at him without speaking and wondered what he was trying to tell her. Who would be this man's enemy? He was the kindest, gentlest man she'd ever met. Even so, if this was the sort of man that ruled their kingdom then she would serve him gladly. She smiled at him. 'Then I will take the oath of loyalty willingly.'

He smiled back, and she offered him another hug which he took in his gentle embrace. She offered him the damp hanky back, too, but he shook his head and indicated she could keep it.

Her eyes flew wide with surprise. 'But ... it must be worth my mother's inn!'

'Oh, it's just a silk hanky,' he replied.

'What's silk?' she asked, turning her third ever possession with admiration and pride.

He laughed a hearty, happy laugh.

'And let's get you out of these rags! What's your mother dressing you kids in these days?'

'Umm ...' She just didn't have the heart to tell him it wasn't her mother that had given her that dress at all.

'Midnera, my queen,' he called to the beautiful old lady who was still by the table. Her face held such a kind smile as he spoke.

'What are you up to now?' she said with a gentle laugh.

'Nothing, nothing at all!' he smiled. 'But see this old thing here they got poor Kialessa in! No, no, this won't do for the King's college.'

Kialessa held her breath. What was he about to do?

'Remember that old outfit Princess Jamine used to wear, when she was down at the lake? Her day clothes, yes?'

The queen smiled again, 'You've a soft heart, my dear.'

'And giving children presents brings me joy,' he replied.

In a few moments a maid was summoned and, in half a breath, she had returned with a bright floral dress, white and gold and blue. It was built with strong, heavy fabric. It had seen little use and fit Kialessa perfectly. They popped her inside a room beside the throne room, and the queen even helped her fit it while they chatted about kings and castles.

She twirled in front of the mirror.

She couldn't help herself. She ran back into the throne room and hugged the king again as he was talking to an exasperated steward. Then she stood back, and curtsied as low as she could go while the steward coughed with embarrassment.

Her king laughed. 'Now Kialessa,' he said in a kind voice, 'I'm such a very busy king, we won't get to speak often. But, make sure you tell the headmistress all about your day. She will tell the steward, who will keep me updated over all your doings. Study hard, young child.'

She frowned openly at that. She did not like that arrangement one bit. The king waited for her to form her thoughts into words, and when they did, she brightened.

'When I learn to write, your majesty, I will send you letters.'

Whatever protest the steward had, it was lost in the king's

royal laughter. 'So be it! Yes, that will please me very much.' Then he whispered close to her ear, 'and you can keep an eye on those bossy tutors of mine!'

He put a finger beside his nose and winked.

She giggled, and he chuckled.

'Your highness,' a messenger announced to the hall. The king looked up.

'Yes?'

'The ambassador from Fae'merel has arrived.'

The king sighed. 'Well, back to work then. Send him in.'

He walked back to his throne and they hurried her out. There, beside the throne on a velvet cushion, was a golden crown, set with a deep purple amethyst flanked by two bright sapphires on either side. The king sat down, and settled the emblem of power on his head.

But before anyone could drag her out, Kialessa pulled herself from the steward's hand and ran across the room to give him one last hug as he sat on his golden chair.

He kissed her forehead, right between the horns. 'You'll do great, I just know it,' he said. 'It might be tough some days. It has to be that way to bring out your best. But you will do great things, for great good, I know.'

Life won't change unless you ask it to.
– From 'The year in jail', by the Tae'anaryn

Then the headmistress took Kialessa to meet the other students. For about the first two moments none of them seemed to notice her horns. They wouldn't stop talking about the dress!

'Wasn't that what Princess Jamine once wore? I saw it at the picnic when I was five …'

'It doesn't really fit her …'

'It simply doesn't suit her complexion …'

She'd been brought up to the alchemic lore study room. There were about thirty students, half the children in her group, and they were almost all humans. Most of them were children of nobles, scholars or wealthy merchants. She'd never seen this many children at once in her entire life. Their looks were a mixture of fear, distrust and open hostility. Kialessa clutched the door frame as though it might protect her from their stares, but stare they did.

The headmistress interrupted the tutor and hushed them all to silence. Then she introduced Kialessa, instructing them all to remember their manners and show kindness.

But Kialessa thought they did not look kind.

'Go child,' she told her, 'take that open seat by the wall.'

The seat was right at the back of the class and Kialessa was grateful for that. Students stared as she passed, and a few moved their chairs well away from her.

'No need for impoliteness!' the headmistress instructed in a firm voice, and then left without looking back.

Kialessa sat down and looked at the hard wooden desk. It was blank, with nothing but a stone tipped stylus for writing. All the other students were copying figures from the board, their styli making small, soft clicking sounds as they wrote on the slate boards they used. But as she sat down she realised she had nothing to write on.

She looked over at the student next to her, a big human boy, and he covered his work with a scowl. Her gaze returned to her desk. It was very thick. Then it dawned on her that it might even be thick enough to hold something in. She pried her fingers under the cover board and was grateful to see it opened up to reveal a large drawer within. Inside there were several cracked and broken sheets of slate. Ruing the noise, she removed the largest one as it scraped and bumped the desk, and almost the whole class stopped to watch. She just bent her head and pretended she was writing, just like the rest of them. Then she dug out a stylus and tried to join in.

     By Dr Joseph Ireland "Dr Joe"

The room itself was too old and boring, and far too cold. As for the lesson, Kialessa found it was tedious and boring. She didn't understand a word of what was going on, and all she could do was copy whatever symbols the tutor was inscribing on the board. She had no idea what they meant, though there were a few Ks; those she knew.

The tutor did light a fire just by looking at it. That was pretty amazing.

But when it came time to check her work he just looked at her slate, his bushy eyebrows raised high. He said nothing, but it looked as if he was thinking, *We've a lot of work to do with you.*

Some other girls giggled at her then, whispering to each other. They were so pretty, dressed in lovely dresses of the latest design, with ribbons of spun gold and silver in their hair. They made a point to take to each task with skill and aplomb, and Kialessa envied their confidence.

Then they almost pushed her flat on her face when it was time to leave, with a fickle, 'Oh sorry', and went giggling on their way.

That was how college went for the first few days, except that the treatment by the other students grew steadily worse. Kialessa had said nothing on the first day, even less on the second, but still they found reasons to whisper about her every chance they got, and to ignore her whenever she tried to speak to them or ask for help.

Eventually Kialessa found the courage to tell the headmistress about the way the other students were treating her, whispering it to her in the quiet one night.

'Have patience, Kialessa. All new students need time to fit in. Remember the old saying: Good things come to those who wait!'

So Kialessa spent the whole week waiting in misery. The days were impossibly long, and the nights unforgivably uncomfortable. There were too many rules to remember, and so she kept forgetting ones she'd heard just after getting in trouble for breaking a few new ones she'd never known. Everybody seemed to be out to get her, and it was obvious that no one wanted her there. In the evenings all the girls would sit together talking about the day. She tried to join in, but they all pushed up next to each other and wouldn't let her find a seat. So, instead, she sat by the window and pretended not to listen to their happy, cheery conversation.

It made her wish she was back home.

Sitting at the window one evening, making small, sorry pictures with her breath across the cold glass, Kialessa listened as the headmistress moved students out one at a time to wash their face and hands in preparation for bed. The moon was covered in clouds and it was dark outside.

'Guess what?' one of the girls said, eyes wide with glee. 'Mother is thinking of buying me that new dress, you know, the one in the high market dressmaker's stall?'

'No!' The others appropriately chorused their cued disbelief.

' 'Tis true, though I hardly need it. Still, 'tis a very pretty thing, all pink and white. Perhaps I will wear it next week,' she boasted. 'I may even let some of you try it on.'

Kialessa knew that someone who would *not* be trying on the new dress would be her. There was no need to ask. It was more than she could stand. She only had *one* dress and *no* friends to share it with. Knowing that just added to the sadness.

Kialessa could not sleep at all that night. She kept having

strange dreams about her home and family, as if someone was trying to tell her something and it kept waking her up. Sometime before midnight, when the moon was over half full in the sky and shyly peeking from between the clouds, she wrapped herself in her only blanket and snuck on her worn shoes. Then she broke the rules and tiptoed out on her silent feet.

At first she did not know where to go in the darkness, so she went wherever the darkness took her. Eventually she walked right up to the inner castle parapets. By then the sky was full of clouds and no one appeared to notice her as she climbed the inner stairs of the giant wall alone and looked out into the darkness.

The night was silent and empty, as empty as her heart.

It is so unfair, she thought. *Here I am, given the opportunity of a lifetime and there is no one to share it with! Even Kiel would be company. At least he would speak to me! How I miss him.*

But as she watched the silent clouds roll by she realised something even more. She hated her life at home. She hated what she would become. She hated knowing she could not read. So she made a promise to herself and the clouds: no matter how bad it got, she would not give up on her education. Anything was better than what she would become if she left and returned to being a slave at her mother's inn. Her mother could never imagine she'd be anything more than a servant, and not a friend to a king. She hadn't even started to write her letter to him yet. She had no *idea* where to begin, and learning to read was so much harder than she'd ever imagined. College was tough, and the constant stares of the crowds were more than she could bear. She was a monster to them; a disease, something to be avoided at all costs. That was what it was like to be a tae'anaryn. That was what it was like to be Kialessa.

Tears rolled down her dusk red cheeks, but still she didn't make a sound. She was not supposed to be up here and if they heard her … But at least the clouds would listen.

She stared out then, her heart as silent as the night, till at last a single wish formed itself in there and she sent it out into the halcyon darkness.

I wish, she thought, *I wish that at least there was someone my age who would talk to me, and maybe help me learn to read.*

But clouds don't talk back.

After a while, Kialessa began to feel numb again inside, and tired enough to perhaps get some sleep before facing another day. She huddled against the cool of the night.

Yes, it is time to go back to bed.

She was just about to climb down the stairs when a strange movement caught her eye. It almost looked as if someone was climbing down the walls of the inner castle.

She had to blink.

It *was* someone, and they were wearing a night grey cloak that hid them very well from the pale light of the covered moon.

Kialessa froze.

This isn't right, she thought.

The cloaked figure worked their way along the inside wall, feeling it with their hands as they went, almost as if they could not see in the darkness at all. This person seemed suspicious, looking around all the time as though they did not want to be seen there.

With great care, and without making a single sound, Kialessa crept along the wall to where she could see what the intruder was doing. She pressed her body to the shadows between the floor and castle wall where they were the darkest, just the way she'd

 By Dr Joseph Ireland "Dr Joe"

worked out how to escape from her mother's constant watch.

Whoever it was had a clear purpose in mind. They crept right up to the inner keep where the king and all his royal servants were no doubt sleeping this late at night. The intruder then went to a stained-glass window and opened it with ease.

Kialessa wondered why that window wasn't locked.

A dim light shone through the glass. It looked like it backed on to the kitchens, or near to it. The intruder then removed a small container in the shape of a saltshaker and, in complete silence, managed to remove the base and began to add a small amount of fine dust to it. Kialessa had a bad feeling she knew exactly what it was: poison.

Kialessa's pulse leapt to a thunderous beat in panic. This was serious. *Someone was trying to poison the king!*

Her mind leapt back to the dream she'd had last week, the night of the dog attack, and she wondered why she hadn't remembered it before. *The King of Lenmer'el must die.* Dream or not, she would not let that happen. She almost screamed out, but then realised the intruder would probably run away in no time. So instead, as quick and as quiet as a mouse, she made her way to an inner wall's tower where the guards could always be found keeping watch.

At least, they were **supposed** to be keeping watch.

She pressed the door open and was glad to see no light fled out, but the noise of the soldiers talking was obvious to her. She looked to see if the intruder had noticed. He was paused, looking about, as though he had.

She crept in and quickly shut the door, racing up the stairs. 'Guards!' she screamed as soon as she saw them. 'Someone is trying to poison –'

'A student!' one of them shouted, and they all leapt up with weapons drawn. 'What're you doing here!' the guard commander scowled.

'Put those away folks, it's just a kid,' Kialessa heard a familiar voice say.

She tried to press past the annoying soldier to see who had spoken, but she held her back with her powerful, adult hand. She was red faced and angry to see her, and hadn't listened at all to what she'd just said. The soldier with the kind voice approached.

'Noe-esk!' Kialessa shouted in relief.

'Put this demon back in her pen,' the soldier spat.

'What a moment,' Noe-esk dared to risk disobeying the girl in charge. 'What is it, young one?'

'I *just* saw an intruder putting something into the king's kitchen. He came from outside, wearing a cloak.'

The room fell silent.

'Are you sure?' Noe-esk asked.

'Yes!' Kialessa replied feeling very indignant. Why would she make something like this up?

The guards were out there so fast they knocked her right on her back and she somehow managed to grab hold of a pot and drag it to the floor as well, shattering it to pieces.

'There he goes!' she heard one of them shout out a moment later from outside. Some bowstrings sung out, but it was followed by cursing, which could only mean the guards had missed.

Kialessa hadn't even finished picking herself up by the time Noe-esk and the other guards had returned. They all looked very serious indeed.

'Come child,' the angry guard commander said, 'we'd better take you to see the steward.'

Kialessa swallowed hard.

***

'You saw *what*?' the steward roared. He was red faced and flustered. 'And what in the gods' names were you doing out in the castle at night?'

Kialessa was silent; he wasn't really asking a question.

'An intruder,' the sergeant said. She was the perfect depiction of politeness in front of the powerful steward. 'She tells us he was wearing a grey cloak. We saw him under the window, but he ran as soon as we took aim. We think he went over the Western wall.'

The steward growled like this was all her fault. 'Is this true, girl?' She nodded, her head whipping up and down in a furious motion.

In the next instant the wizard burst in, a dark blue whirl of electricity crackling around his staff. 'What has happened?' he said, voice raised in alarm.

'An intruder,' the steward replied in a far calmer voice. 'He escaped over the western wall. The little tae'anaryn girl was the first to sight him.'

'Whatever was she doing out of bed?' the wizard asked, switching off the staff.

In the next moment the king's high priestess wandered in, flustered, but alert. She was a plump old dwarven woman, with small eyes and soft hands. She'd likely come from the religious shrine she tended next to the king's throne room. 'I had a premonition just now, is the king all right? What has happened?' she said, her voice forceful yet gentle.

'An intruder,' the wizard replied.

'I thought as much. Though the omens this week spoke of the protector tonight. Is the king safe?'

'Yes, yes, of course,' the steward began, 'and I assure you I am up to my task –'

He was cut off suddenly as the king's captain burst in. He too was an older man, but still strong and energetic, with a deep barrelled chest and rippling with well-exercised muscles. He was armed with more swords and axes than Kialessa would ever have thought possible to carry. He had a long, dark red moustache, and the look on his face was one of a professional willing to die for his king at any moment.

'**Where is the intruder!?!**' he yelled.

'He's escaped,' the steward sighed in a tired voice.

This is an awful lot of commotion, Kialessa thought, about ready to giggle. It was like a reunion of all the important people in the castle.

'Who saw him?'

They pointed at her and the sergeant.

'Actually …' the sergeant said, pointing just at her.

'What is she doing out of bed at this hour?' the captain demanded.

Honestly, Kialessa thought, *they are more worried about a student being out of bed than someone trying to poison the King!*

And that was when the king walked in, wearing his red woollen nightclothes. Everyone snapped to attention.

Kialessa yawned. She couldn't help it. His nightclothes just looked so cosy and warm.

'Evening all,' the king said, the calm amid the storm, and took a drink the steward offered. 'Cool night to be out discussing things, isn't it?'

'Your Grace,' the captain said, 'it may not be safe to be out here. An intruder was spotted near the keep tonight.'

'Really?' he said. Clearly, he had missed the news. 'By whom?'

'One of the students,' the priestess explained, indicating Kialessa.

The King looked at her, 'Really? Young Kialessa, whatever were you doing out of bed this late in the evening?' he asked, his voice gentle.

Everyone waited for her to answer.

Suddenly, Kialessa wasn't feeling indignant anymore. She was terrified. It was late and she was tired. How could she tell him that she hated his college; that no one spoke to her, and that she'd been out there so she could cry and not be seen?

The king looked at her with kindness in his eyes, and called her over. Holding her hand with gentle affection, he offered her the water he was drinking. She took it with gratitude, hoping that her nervousness didn't suddenly burst out into tears once more.

'I went for a walk,' she explained in a whisper.

'Child, you know the rule –' the steward begun to lecture.

The king glanced at him, and he fell silent. 'You decided to go for a walk,' he repeated.

Kialessa could feel all her sorrow and tiredness surfacing again. How she would have given anything for one chance to be tucked up in her stupid little bed in the dormitory, rather than standing around with all these gawking, demanding adults!

'How is college, Kialessa?' he asked.

That was all it took. She bit her lip to stop from crying, but the tears escaped freely anyway.

He hugged her and then set her up on a little wooden chair. 'There, there,' he said. The other adults flustered over other matters for a few moments.

'I do wish people were nicer to me,' she whispered to him. A moment later a pair of soldiers arrived.

'Captain,' the sergeant began. She was breathing heavily as though she'd been running all night, and she glared at Kialessa with an annoyed look on her face. 'We've searched the area and found footprints but nothing else. However, I believe the child mentioned this,' she said, producing the saltshaker.

The wizard examined it, running the salt between his fingers and touching the smallest grains to his tongue. 'Saltweed,' he proclaimed.

They all gasped.

'Saltweed?' the king asked.

'Not deadly,' the steward explained, 'but it weakens the will of any who consume it.'

'Whatever for?' the king asked.

'Clouding the judgement,' the priestess explained. 'Dishonest traders sometimes use it to make customers unwary, or gamblers more foolish.'

'I don't think any trader we know would risk their lives to poison the king, unless it was particularly profitable,' the wizard ensaged. 'I think it much more likely that this is an act by someone who intends you further harm.'

                    By Dr Joseph Ireland "Dr Joe"

'Then it is the precursor to another attack?' the captain said.

'A long-term plan by the looks of things,' the wizard said.

The wizard then handed the shaker to the priestess. 'Can you see who interfered with it?'

She closed her eyes in silent prayer, then shook her head.

The wizard continued, 'As I suspected, it must be very well veiled. Also, it appears to have a mild but clever enchantment on it. It is enspelled to be outside the perception of the kitchen staff. I imagine they would have absent-mindedly applied the salt on their way to the king's table, not even remembering it.'

'Then the poison would have been applied *after* the priests had checked the food for danger?' the steward said.

'Indeed,' the priestess looked chagrined. 'Your highness, I apol –' she began.

The king waved her to silence as if it was just not important anymore. 'Forgive yourself. It was obviously a well-executed plan. And Kialessa,' he said, 'I feel I should thank you, though you were not supposed to be out of bed. You may have just saved us a great deal of … inconvenience.'

Everyone was very quiet for a while, but Kialessa didn't care what they said. By the sound of things, she was not in any real trouble for being out of bed, because she'd just saved their lives or something. She just wanted to curl up with some nice woollen nightclothes like the king's. But there was a little ball of happiness deep inside her heart now. She had helped the King of Lenmer'el!

She *was* good for something.

'We'd better double the guard,' the captain said. 'And tighten up security! If there's a threat on the king's life, it is a threat on the kingdom!'

'Now hang on a moment,' the steward disagreed, 'let's not go getting the citizenry all worked up. It's not uncommon for Saltweed to be used to sully the minds of those negotiating business deals. This may have simply been a foolish attempt by a visiting merchant to secure an overpriced payment. It may not have even been directed at the king.'

'That is a sound assumption,' the wizard agreed.

'I fear otherwise,' the priestess said with confidence. 'As I have told you before, the portents speak of a season of darkness on this land, punctuated by moments of blinding light. I fear this incident is just a forerunner of things to come.'

Everyone was quiet in their thoughts for a moment. Kialessa yawned again.

The King looked at her and smiled. 'Good point, Kialessa, it is late. Captain, check into security but let's do this quietly, no need to alarm everyone just yet.'

'Yes, your highness!'

'And as for you, little Kialessa … Kialessa?'

But Kialessa had had enough. The adults were handling things now as far as she could tell, and so she had flung herself onto one of the steward's sheepskin rugs. It was so warm and woolly, not at all like the thin sheets they gave her to sleep on. With both eyes closed, she just listened to what the adults were saying.

'Steward,' the King whispered, no doubt thinking she was already asleep, 'make sure you instruct the guard that if Kialessa is ever found wondering around, she is to be told to move on but not arrested, in case some more good comes of it.'

'But your grace -!' he began a whispered protest.

The king wouldn't let him speak. 'And please make sure the students are reminded of the need to welcome everyone to my college. They know what is right. Perhaps they just need a little … reminder.'

'Indeed, my king,' he replied, his voice a softer tone.

Kialessa smiled to herself and peeked out from her vantage point. The king and his soldiers were busy, and the wizard and captain had already left. There was no-one to see her now. No one except the high priestess, who gave her a knowing smile as though she was quite aware that Kialessa was listening to the whole thing.

The priestess nodded. *You've done well, little one, now sleep on till the late dawn,* she seemed to say. In a moment, Kialessa found herself given over quite completely to the need to sleep. It was an amazing thing, what these priests of faith could do on this world …

She never noticed them carrying her back to bed, rug and all. She didn't even notice they let her sleep-in till almost midday, though she **did** notice how they let her keep the little rug which warmed her bed so much more in the coming nights. She slept well that night, though she did dream of Kiel and her parents. It was as if he was trying to say something to her, though by the morning she couldn't remember what it was.

The next day the headmistress read out an announcement, from the steward himself, to the entire college.

'Dear students, greetings and salutations from the king's steward. It has come to my attention that some of you may not be treating students new to this college with the same dignity and camaraderie as your older friends. It would give His Majesty King Dunnkan, whom we honour and serve, great comfort to know you were helping other students to feel welcomed and safe in his college, and that you were treating all students, regardless of upbringing, religion or *race*, with the kindness His Majesty shows us all each day. Sincerely, the steward.'

It actually worked, more or less. Students were nicer to her, at least most of the time. They would let her sit at their tables and didn't giggle when she walked past. They still tended to not answer her questions, and she soon realised she would never get much more from college till she learnt how to read for herself.

'Good things come to those who wait,' the old headmistress had said.

But nothing comes to those who don't wish! Kialessa now thought.

In the following weeks she snuck out often to watch the stars, to cool her hands in the breeze, or to simply listen to other people while they shared their secrets in the quiet night. It was a freedom that helped keep her happy in a college without friends.

They never did find out why the steward had written that letter.

The Wizard's Apprentice

There is one question I've never been able to answer, at least to my satisfaction, and it regards a certain event many, many years ago. So, tell me, if you are wiser than I once was: is it all right to steal to help a friend?

Ruminations of the lost wizard, p 147

From that point on Kialessa was determined to succeed at college. Even if it took time, she would succeed. She was going to learn how to read. She was going to do whatever it took!

She had to beg, but the next day the tutor finally gave her a parchment: a list of words she was supposed to know. They made no sense to her; no sense at all. Neither did the little pictures beside each word. She padded down the pathway till she came to the steps and followed the sound of students playing. They'd been let out of their heraldry and historical lore class early. It was late afternoon, and they were all out at the large field where trade caravans would often arrive to promote their wares. A huge tree provided a little shade, while the students skipped rope, chatted, or chased each other around.

Kialessa's heart ached to be part of one of those games, but there was always a problem: you needed a friend, and she had none. Some of them saw her, standing alone by the stone pillars of the arch, dressed in yellow and blue and white. None of them approached her.

Were they still afraid?

Kialessa looked around. There, sitting a few paces away, was a small boy she'd seen but never noticed before. He might have been about her age, but he was very small. Along his neck tiny dragon scales were barely visible. His fingers ended almost in claws, not fingernails, and they were holding a book in his hand. He rocked back and forth as he read.

Reading. He was understanding the language in a book!

I will have to make him my first friend, she thought. *But how to begin?*

She took a breath, made a wish, and said the first thing that popped into her head. 'Hi,' she said invitingly, her voice catching just a little in her throat.

He looked up at her, with yellowish-hazel eyes shaped like a cat's. No wonder none of the other children were playing with him. But he only glanced her way and then went straight back to reading his book.

'What'cha reading?' she asked, trying to get him to speak to her. He didn't.

'Is it a book?' She moved closer; she wasn't going to give up yet. He looked up her, his eyes angry and impatient. He really looked as if he didn't want to be disturbed, and as if to emphasise it he stuck out his tongue. It was forked and blue.

She poked her tongue at him too, forked and reddish brown. Hers was much longer.

He smiled then, and she smiled back.

'My name is Kialessa,' she said, beginning to feel more confident now, and sat beside him on the stone steps in friend distance.

'I know,' he said. 'You came in last week. You're a tae'anaryn.'

He said it like it was a scientific fact and not like a disease.

That was good.

He held that book pretty close.

'What are you reading?' she asked him again.

'Words,' he said with a cheeky smile.

'What do they say?' she asked, not put off by his rudeness yet. She figured that while he still talked to her there was a chance they'd become friends one day.

He smiled and then moved so she could see the strange words that ran along the page. He read, '*Panton said in oratio draco sanus profundus.*'

'What?' she said.

'It's dragon speech.' He smiled to himself.

It wasn't even Emerellian, the language they all spoke. He was reading in another language. Her mouth fell open in surprise and envy.

'You're reading a *different language?*'

'Oh, it's not hard,' he boasted, sounding arrogant, though he probably didn't mean to. 'I speak and read four languages. Elven and troll as well. And I'm learning *Iaith yr awyr*. That's the language of the beings from the elemental dimension of air, you know. I like the air element, but perhaps that's because my grandfather was a half star dragon-'

'Wait a moment,' Kialessa interrupted, too impressed for words. '*Four* languages? What kind of genius are you?'

He smiled and then looked out at the others playing. He dug his heel in the dust at his feet. 'The lonely kind, I suppose.'

'They don't like it when other children look different, do they?'

'What? No, that's not it,' he said. 'My father makes me study for four hours longer than anybody else. I use up my break time studying so that I can make up stories after the sun sets. Now everybody just leaves me alone.'

'Oh,' Kialessa said.

The boy continued. 'I'm part dragon. People like dragons. They don't play with you because you're a tae'anaryn. People don't like ...'

'Tae'anaryl,' she finished for him.

'No. Demons. The Tae'anaryl have a demon for a parent, don't you know? It's in Loremaster Trax's guide to the outer planes. My dad has the only copy this side of Emerel.'

But Kialessa was upset at this suggestion. 'My father always told me that one of my ancestors was wounded fighting with a demon in the Great War. I'm descended from a hero.'

'Really? We'll I've never heard of that happening, but perhaps it is so.'

She was a bit hurt, though she could tell he hadn't meant it.

       By Dr Joseph Ireland "Dr Joe"

Even so, he may have just told her something she really didn't want to know.

He looked about, probably not sure why she was being quiet.

Then he buried his head back in his book.

'What ya reading?' she said, again. It felt as if she'd already asked him this a zillion times.

'What? Oh, this is Mitimax's guide to the creatures of the great desert. He was a desert dragon you know, and my great grandfather won this off him in a contest of riddles. Never go in a contest of riddles with a star dragon!'

'Dragon?' Kialessa interrupted, sitting up straight. 'Does that mean you can breathe fire, or acid?'

He looked sad. 'No, I don't think I ever will. Father says my elementarum is dysfunctional. It's an extra organ only dragons and half dragons have that produces their breath.'

'Where did you learn all this?' she said. He was a wealth of knowledge.

'Books! I *love* books!' he said, clutching the one he had to his chest and fairly trembling in excitement. His eyes were dilated orbs of arcane enthusiasm.

Yes, this boy loves books. She laughed.

'How I wish I could read!' she mused out loud.

He looked shocked. 'You can't read!' he sputtered. 'How can you not read?'

'My parents never taught me. I don't think they can read either.'

'But King Dunnkan's grandfather made reading lessons compulsory for all citizens sixty-four years ago. How come they didn't learn to read?'

2 This boy loves books

'I just don't know.'

'Look,' he said, scrawling in the dust. 'Here's how you spell your name in Emerellian. Just like this.'

'Oh, I can write my name.'

'Well, here's how to spell it in ancient, it sounds like an ancient name. Now you have to be careful because translations are rarely literal.' He scribbled in the sand. 'Lessa is a verb, and it means 'to set free' and Kia –'

 By Dr Joseph Ireland "Dr Joe"

'Actually,' Kialessa said, 'I'd be just as happy if I could read Emerellian.'

'Well,' he said, rubbing his chin, 'I need to study. I'm sure the headmistress will have some early texts for you to peruse. Maybe at the library?'

'Is that where they keep books?' she asked. Maybe that was where the steward worked?

He looked at her like she was from another world. 'Ahh, I don't think I can help you. I need to read.'

'Too busy, huh?'

'Something like that.'

'What would make you less busy?'

'Oh, if I had a better tutor!' he replied.

She was determined to do whatever it took to get him to teach her to read, even if he was the busiest person in all the world. And he was the first other young person to speak with her sensibly.

He continued, 'They only ever send the apprentices to teach the young wizards like me,' he said. 'If I could get just five moments with the castle mage, I'm sure I can impress him. Then maybe he'd take me on as an apprentice. Five moments with his experience would be worth a day with one of the unskilled tutors. I just have to, but he's never given me the time.'

Kialessa smiled. She knew how to get a wizard's attention. If there was one thing her mother had taught her, it was how to get people's attention. She used to boast about how she got whatever she wanted, even if it wasn't in a very … helpful way.

'We just need to find something he wants.' She grabbed his hand and pulled him to his feet, his book almost slipping from his grasp.

'Hey!'

'C'mon, what did you say your name was?'

'I didn't. It's Piex.'

'That's a nice name,' she said.

They chatted while she dragged him around the castle. She knew where she was heading. There was a window outside a certain room she'd passed on her tour to see the king, and inside that room was the answer to her and her new friend's quest. Kialessa held her head up like she was supposed to be there, and none of the guards stopped them as they wandered along, far from where the other students were playing.

They crept through the garden outside the wizard's study. Kialessa found herself thinking that if they wanted to keep people out, they really shouldn't have planted such good, thick hedges right under the windows. They were very good for hiding behind.

This was the place.

'Kialessa,' Piex said in a worried voice, 'we shouldn't be here! Where have you taken me?'

Kialessa knelt down in front of him and smiled as she watched him, wringing his hands together in worry, a little like Kiel. 'Look, Piex, I've got an idea. I think to get the wizard's attention we need to help him in some way. So, I'm going to find something that he wants and then we find it for him. Then, when he asks us about it you can show him your magic. Sounds like a plan, right?'

He looked really worried. 'Why don't we just ask him?'

'Has that ever worked before?'

He shook his head.

'Trust me,' she smiled, remembering the things her cunning mother had taught her. 'Sometimes you just have to help people out to get their attention. And sometimes you have to help them in ways they didn't even know you could. Help them before asking for a favour. This'll change everything.'

She felt bold, even for herself. But it felt better to be making her own choices instead of waiting for someone else to turn up and fix things.

The upper windows were open, which was good, but they were all far too visible from the lawn to be safe. She tried the lower ones, but they were all locked from the inside. But Kialessa wasn't worried. She'd prepared for this. Along their way she'd picked up a reed from the lily pond. It was long, thin and very strong. She folded it into a loop and, with practiced skill, snuck it between the window and the sill. She worked her way along the edge till she found the latch. It was what her father had taught her to do if she'd ever been locked out at night. Kialessa smiled to herself. She remembered how her mother was always losing the keys to customers' rooms and needed Kialessa to pop open the locks for her so she could clean them.

This lock, however, was a bit tricky, and it took almost two moments while Piex fretted, but soon enough she heard the happy pop of a window latch opening.

Honestly. You'd think wizards would have better window security than that! she thought.

She crawled inside. The entire room was well organised. The books and scrolls were neat and filled up an entire wall. There were dozens of glass jars and apparatus along the other wall and, under the window, just where she came in, there was a great desk made of a single sculpted piece of wood.

And there was the wizard.

He was sitting in a great chair, turned towards a grand fireplace where a deep red fire danced.

Kialessa's heart was pounding in her chest. She didn't dare to move. She'd hoped he was out, but perhaps it was better that she knew where he was. Provided it even was the castle's elven wizard …

Piex peered in the window, but Kialessa indicated he needed to get down. He looked around like he could spend all week in there, and his head lowered until at last his reluctant eyes disappeared below the windowsill.

She crept up to the wizard's chair without making a sound – at least she was very good at that – and walked around it till she could see his face. He was asleep, that was for sure.

Then with a gasp Kialessa heard unexpected voices out in the hall. She tried to hide herself beside the chair. If she was caught here, it could be her last day at the college.

But as luck would have it no one came in.

What am I here for again? she wondered, but then remembered: To see what a wizard needed. Perhaps if she took a book, or a jar of goo? She could then offer it to him when he found he was lacking one. No, he'd be too clever for that trick. Besides, it would be wrong to steal. She looked around. There were some apprentice wands and a parchment on the table. She bent her head to examine the parchment. It looked like some kind of list. She saw that a number of the items were ticked off, all except three.

With luck, they were things a wizard needed.

Kialessa looked around till she found another piece of

parchment, scrawled together and tossed into a waste basket. Perfect. Then she looked for a quill. She found one, resting in a clear crystal jar on the desk, just where you'd expect to find one.

But before she could touch it a strange creature uncurled itself from around some books where it had been watching her the whole time, watching from invisibility. It stood up in front of that quill.

It was a pocket dragon.

It had beautiful purple and gold scales, and large dragonfly wings. It was no bigger than the palm of her hand, but she could see it had some nasty sharp teeth. Its body was long and its tail even longer. It stood up on its hind legs and sniffed the air towards her.

The wizard stirred but did not rise.

She needed that quill. Barely daring to breath, she reached her hand out and the little dragon sniffed at it, then pulled away. She reached towards the quill and touched it. The dragon sniffed the air towards her as if curious, watching what her hand was doing. Kialessa sighed in relief as the crystal jar filled with a deep blue ink as she begun to remove the quill.

Without warning the little dragon jumped on her wrist, making a cute little 'mmm-haa?' noise.

Kialessa froze and almost squealed in panic, but the wizard didn't stir. She needed that quill, so she spoke the only secret password she knew. 'Please,' she whispered to the dragon, 'I need this for a friend.'

3 The pocket dragon guards his master's quill

The dragon hopped down off her wrist and came to look over the parchments. Kialessa breathed a great huge sigh of relief, as quiet as she possibly could. With great care she copied the strange names that weren't ticked on the list. Then she replaced the quill and folded the parchment into her floral dress.

Kialessa watched as the dragon returned to its perch on the books. She nodded her thanks and she thought she saw the little half insect nod in return. It made her smile.

She tiptoed to the window again and, with less noise than a shadow, crept out. She didn't let Piex talk as they slunk from the wizard's study and made their way along the grass. As soon as

     By Dr Joseph Ireland "Dr Joe"

some guards had passed by, she dragged him by the hand and started walking normally along the corridors of stone.

But Piex was still creeping.

'What are you doing?' she said.

'We're sneaking.'

'Not anymore. What, you want people to suspect you?'

He looked around and straightened up. 'Sorry, I've just never stolen anything before.'

'Stolen?' she said, surprised and a little amused.

'Yea, that's why, right? You stole something that we plan to return to the wizard in a few hours and then he'll have the time to listen to me. Then I'll show him my skill at wizardry and maybe ask him some questions. Right?'

'No,' Kialessa said, making her voice sound shocked by the suggestion. 'He's a wizard. He'd know who took his stuff.'

Piex looked doubtful. Perhaps he knew something she didn't?

She rolled her eyes. 'Look, I didn't steal anything.'

'Right,' he said in a sarcastic voice.

'Unless you count stealing things that their owners get to keep.'

'What?'

'Information, silly. It's a riddle.'

'What? Oh. Oh! A riddle! Oh, now I get it!' He laughed a crooked and nasal laugh that made her begin to regret she'd said something he found funny.

He seemed genuinely tickled. 'Take what owners get to keep. That's such a good one! I'll have to tell father.'

'Maybe you'd better not mention that riddle to your father.'

'What? Oh yeah, right!' he said. 'So, what was it that you took?'

'This.' She handed him the paper.

'Oh, it's elven. Wow, you don't even read elven … that's very good copying. Wait a second, is that the letter 'e' or 'é'? Oh, it's '*menthe poivrée*' so it has to be …' he prattled on.

'What is it?'

'Seems to be some ingredients for a potion or something. Here, the common names are toadswool, that's a plant, eyes of newt – wow, they're common – and golden peppermint.'

'Golden peppermint?' Kialessa asked.

'Yeah, it's really hard to get good quality golden peppermint.'

'That's that herb you use to season the winter goose, right?' she said.

'Well, you can, but like most things it also has magical properties, very useful –'

'What are you talking about?' she interrupted. 'It's not rare, I saw some up here on the way to the palace a week ago. It was really thick and bushy.'

'Bushy? Really? Where?' Piex said as his face lit up with wonder. 'There is no way there'd be golden peppermint just lying around without the wizard knowing.'

'It was just outside the castle where we stopped to let a trading caravan past.'

Piex was silent for a moment and then said, 'They'll never let us out of the castle at this hour. It's late in the afternoon.'

'Let's do it anyway.' She smiled. She didn't really think they'd get in very much trouble for being a little late, and Kialessa couldn't bear the thought of suffering another day not being able to read and join in with what was going on at the college.

They rushed down towards the castle gate. However, the castle guards were just as helpful as Piex had said. She was beginning to despair that they'd never get out.

Suddenly a voice said, 'Tae'anaryn child, what are you doing at the gate this late hour?' It was Noe-esk.

'Good gentle!' she said, unable to believe her luck. 'We've an important little errand to run for the wizard. We need to get some golden peppermint from a little way outside the gates.'

'Really? Where is it?'

'About ten moments down the road.'

He looked at the setting sun 'No time for …' then the kind soldier sighed at Kialessa's eager and enthusiastic expression. '… unless we take Riumi.'

She cheered with delight, and in a moment she and Piex were clutching Noe-esk tightly as Riumi ran at full speed. The evening wind ripped past her face and chilled her clothes. It was terrifying, so she squealed in excitement till the fear passed. The journey took about three moments. She found the plants in the failing light and hurried down to the water. She grabbed up as many as she could hold in one hand.

Piex was amazed. 'That's good quality golden peppermint.'

'What's all this for?' Noe-esk asked suspiciously.

'The wizard,' Kialessa said again, and Noe-esk gave an understanding nod in reply. She smiled to herself. Perhaps youth were often sent out on little errands.

The other two ingredients were a little easier to come by. The markets were shut, so at Piex's suggestion Kialessa thumped on the head gardener's door until someone answered. An old woman's voice told them to come back in the morning.

'It's for the wizard,' Kialessa said.

'What, that old boot?' the woman's voice said. 'What'd he be wanting this late hour?'

'Toadswool, that's a plant, and, please, if you have any eyes of newt?'

'Eyes of newt? Seem to recall a messenger picking up a jar from the animarium across the way …' The door opened to reveal a plump old woman in a nightdress, squinting against the approaching darkness.

Kialessa was worried the old woman might become suspicious, 'I guess he needs newt eyes again, already. We can pay you this,' she said, and offered her a little embroidered hankie the King had given her. This was really important!

The woman's eyes lit up, but then they softened. 'No dear, that will not be necessary. I'll just put it on his account.'

Kialessa smiled to herself that she got to keep her little treasure, but Piex's mouth had dropped open with surprise.

'That's a very generous offer to be helpful with a problem that isn't yours,' he muttered.

'I don't mind helping a friend,' she said. 'Besides, I really need to learn how to read!'

He looked thoughtful.

The old woman returned a moment later with their supplies, and they ran off towards the castle. It was beginning to get quite dark and Kialessa assumed they'd be in trouble soon. Then a pair of armed and daunting guards stopped them just as they were about to get back to the wizard's study.

Kialessa just held out the plant in one hand and the bottles in the other. 'It's for the wizard,' she said, a serious look on her face.

They nodded and let them pass!

'I can't believe we just got away with that!' Piex whispered, but he became quiet once more as they ascended the wizard's stairs.

'You ready?' she said.

His face became white with fear. He put his hand to his chest and started to breathe in rapid, shallow, rasping breaths.

'I can't do it,' he said.

Kialessa looked at him. If he failed, he'd never teach her how to read. But he looked so afraid! How could she help him find the courage to live his dream of facing the wizard and showing him his skills?

'You want to be a wizard, don't you?'

'Yes,' he replied in a voice that was weak and unbelieving.

'You want to be taught by the best?'

He looked down for a moment, then replied much in a much stronger voice, 'Yes.'

She put her hand on his arm, genuinely sympathetic for his struggle. She told him something King Dunnkan had once told her. 'You'll do great things, for great good, I know.'

He smiled. He pulled himself up, and with growing courage took the ingredients from her to present them himself. The wizard, it seemed, was waiting for them as soon as they knocked at his door.

'Young ones, come in. It's already past sunfall, and you would not want to be caught outside this hour, would you?'

Before Kialessa could reply, Piex spoke up. When he did, his timid little boy voice was gone, and he spoke like a brave young wizard's apprentice. *'Ego appologise,'* he said in dragon speech, *'audivi te aliqua necessitate reagentia.'*

'Adveho!' the wizard replied in their mysterious language, and then continued to speak in Emerellian. 'And what ingredients do you have for me this night, young ones, that is worth risking the wrath of those that keep you?'

They entered the neat and organised study once more.

'Only these,' Piex announced with pride. 'Toadswool, eyes of newt and golden peppermint.'

The great wizard's eyebrows shot up in surprise and disbelief. 'That's a curious combination, youngling. I'm wondering where you got such a list?'

'I have ... clever friends.' Piex smiled.

The wizard smiled at Kialessa, and she sighed in relief to see he was not angry. Then she saw the pocket dragon curled up on his hat, right near his ear. The Wizard looked at it for a moment and then winked at her. Perhaps he wasn't sleeping after all?

'Now, eye of newt I was able to procure this afternoon,' the wizard said, 'but how did you come by toadswool?'

'The gardener's wife keeps a broad array of herbs,' Piex said with confidence.

'Really? I was unaware, and I've lived here over one hundred and fifty years.'

'Perhaps it is as Generonix the sage describes. The pace of human culture is with such rapidity that the familiar becomes strange in only a few years –' Piex began a bold lecture.

'I am aware of the writings of Generonix,' the wizard interrupted with a stern stare. 'What makes me extremely curious is your claim to golden peppermint. A cutting of the quality I require must usually be brought in from the herbarium at the capital Emerel.'

'There's a heap of it ten moments outside the city gate,' Kialessa boasted, pushing the plant under his nose.

He looked at it studiously. Then, his eyes grew round. 'Firm, saporous leaves … wide, strong stems … Why, children, this far surpasses the dried cuttings I'm lucky to get from anywhere else. Outside the gate you say?'

'Yes,' they chorused.

'Good! Take my hands, then! Young girl, can you form a firm picture in your mind of the exact location as you saw it most recently?'

'Why of course,' she said, doing her best. She and Piex held the wizard's hands, and Kialessa could feel her friend trembling in fear and anticipation. Suddenly –

Crack, *whoosh*!

The whole study disappeared, and they found themselves standing outside, right next to the patch of golden peppermint.

They'd been teleported!

The wizard's purple stone burst into a bright white light. 'Come! Show me the golden peppermint!'

Kialessa stood back smiling while Piex showed the wizard where they'd found the plant. He grinned with delight. The wizard then summoned the entire guard from the gate and instructed them to pull out torches and quarter off the area. It wasn't happening fast enough, so he used his magic to make the end of one of their spears glow like a torch.

Kialessa couldn't help it; she giggled with delight. She and

Piex jumped for joy.

'Now, young ones, back inside for those so young!' the wizard ordered.

'Sir, if you please,' Piex begged with as much courage as he had. 'There's something I very much want to show you.'

The wizard looked at them, and for a long moment Kialessa was convinced the powerful mage would not have time for them. However, looking about, he seemed satisfied that the guards were doing their job well enough not to need him to supervise them further.

'Very well then,' he said. 'You've saved me many weeks of waiting, clever boy. I can give you at least five moments.'

And with that, he teleported them all back inside his study. 'Now, youngling, what is it you wanted to show me?' the wizard said, as he sat down like an emperor on his chair.

Then Piex turned white with fear. The little boy looked at Kialessa, nervousness streaming from him. She knew he'd been planning this moment for many seasons and now that it was here, his mind had probably gone completely blank.

'You can do it!' Kialessa whispered.

He took a breath. 'If it would please you, honoured Sir, I'd like to show you my wizardry.'

'Very well, what forms?'

'Figments … and a sonorate.'

'Ah,' the wizard sighed, 'from the Undanium and Curatium halls of magic. Very well, youngling, show me your skill in the science of wizardry.'

The young dragon boy drew a deep breath. Kialessa could feel the air around him twingle as he commanded the magic

   By Dr Joseph Ireland "Dr Joe"

hidden there and, using powerful incantations in the silence of his mind, to shape them.

Kialessa had been taught that very few had the wisdom to become a wizard, even fewer to become great wizards, unless they were particularly gifted. Piex, it appeared, was gifted in the extreme.

The lights were amazing, flowing at one with a song she'd never heard. It was simple, sweet, and beautiful. Piex even managed a clever countermelody for the light and airy music. The sounds were *amazing*. She did not know he had such innate mastery of magic! The lights danced and merged, and in their colours, symbols of a language she'd never seen flowed and formed in a thousand hues of blue and white and grey. She did not want the music to end.

But it did and, as it finished, the young mage took a deep breath.

The old wizard did not smile.

Piex turned to leave. 'Thank you, sir,' he whispered, a tear choked in his voice.

'No, no, don't go! I'm just … that was *incredible*.'

A bright smile lit up Piex's face, and little silver tears danced at the edges of his hope filled eyes.

The wizard cleared his throat and tried to speak normally. 'Air speech, I see, from the script, and the music, too, I gather?'

'A lullaby,' Piex explained.

'Well-rehearsed boy. Very well-rehearsed. You display a mastery of concentration and skill worthy of the … well, the very well trained. Who is your tutor here?'

'Tis Marchan, sir.'

'That boy? No, no, that will simply not do. Here,' he said and reached up to his bookshelf. 'Take this. This is *Proof and Refutations of the Hall of Undanium*. It's gnome work – no surprise. And this I think you'll like. It's *A History of the Beings of the Air* by the troll sage, Chatuk. Heard of him? Expect not. Troll sages never accrue the fame their work deserves. And this,' he said, pulling yet another work from the top shelf. *Academiclees: The Study of Modern Magic.* You should have a copy, but this has my personal study notes inside.'

Piex was speechless. Kialessa hit him on the arm to snap him out of his daze.

'Th … thank …' he stammered.

'Thank you!' Kialessa finished for him.

'Thank you! Thank you, honoured mage. A thousand –' Piex blustered.

'Silence youngling!' the wizard ordered, serious once more. 'A wizard's voice is *not* to be wasted.'

Piex clamped his jaws shut with an obedient *ponk!*

'You'll not be seeing that kind, yet… untalented tutor apprentice of mine, Marchan, again, you hear? You are to report to me at dawn. I can no doubt spare five moments of my time to hear of your studies. You've some talent, boy. I'm sorry we've let it go unseen so long. And, we must arrange to have you show your magic to the king!'

Piex went pale once more.

'But not tonight,' the wizard smiled. 'Go to bed, children. I'll send a messenger before you.'

'Thank you,' Kialessa said.

Piex didn't speak till he was at the study door. He then

turned; three large books pressed to his chest. '*Dominus, nox noctis.*' He bowed.

The wizard smiled. '*Alumno.* And, young lady, please make sure you close the window on your next unannounced visit to my study.'

She and Piex looked at each other in wide mouthed surprise but could say no more as the door swung shut of its own accord. After all, he was a master wizard.

They turned and walked down the darkened stairs.

'I guess with all those books you won't have much time to teach me how to read after all,' Kialessa said with a sad frown to Piex as they wandered back to the dormitories.

'By the time I'm finished with you,' the apprentice wizard boasted, smiling mischievously, 'you'll be deciphering the texts of a thousand different worlds.'

The Prayerful Warrior

I have often been asked if there is a right way to pray. I give only one answer: sincerely.

Darrix the Prayerful. 'Reflections'

Life at the collage soon became routine. Kialessa would study while Piex read, and together they would watch the other youth play. The girls were nicer to her now, and some of them even helped her out once in a while. But usually, Kialessa was studying so hard that she almost forgot the room full of girls that, for the most part, ignored her. None of them had laughed when they finally realised she was learning to read, at least not to her face, and not especially since the headmistress had given them such a withering stare they'd almost burst into tears once when one of them did mention it.

 By Dr Joseph Ireland "Dr Joe"

But apart from Piex few of the boys paid her any attention, unless it was to tease her. They would laugh at her behind her back, or throw things at her when the tutors weren't looking.

But then there was Darrix. He was different. He was at least two years older than her, tall and very handsome. He was probably the most popular boy in college; always surrounded by a circle of friends. All the girls talked about him in the evenings, though Kialessa thought it all stupid for girls to have nothing else to do but talk about boys.

Yet even the tutors liked Darrix. They would call on him to carry books or break up fights. And when they wanted a question answered correctly, they'd usually ask Darrix. He was the son of a wealthy merchant who'd struck it rich mining the nearby hills. Everyone expected Darrix to become a great warrior one day. His older brother and sister were already respected additions to the king's guard, and Darrix was showing signs of becoming a strong and skilled soldier one day as well. He was easily the match of the oldest boys in their class and beat them regularly in training. Everyone talked about him making captain before twenty when they thought he wasn't listening, and often when they thought he was.

Yet there was a gentle, and far more mature, side to him that Kialessa didn't see in other boys. On her fourth week of college one of the other smaller boys her age snatched a piece of paper from her. It was one Piex had given her with letters on it for her to memorise.

'Hey!' she shouted. Then she decided to speak nicely at first, though her eyes were already glowing red. She just hoped they were playing and didn't realise they were upsetting her.

'Please give my paper back,' she said in an almost friendly

voice. She held her breath to keep calm.

Piex was already slinking away.

The boy looked at the paper and snarled. 'She can't even read!' The other boys laughed.

'So?' she shouted. He was being mean, and he knew it.

'You're *stupid*,' he said right to her face.

She wanted to hit him but decided against it. Besides, there were five or six of his friends laughing at her as well. She was about to scream at him, to tell him in no uncertain terms to give her paper back when, suddenly, he scrunched the piece of paper up and threw it to one of them.

'Keepings off the half-demon!' he jeered.

'Keepings off! Keepings off!' His friends joined in.

Kialessa didn't move, but just looked at him, threat glowering in her eyes. She wanted her piece of paper back. She wanted to learn how to read.

'What's the matter half-demon?' he jeered. 'Too quick for ya?'

She was about to knock his feet out from under him, even if it did mean the other boys might beat her, when another voice cut in.

'Hey boys,' it said, 'remember she's new here. Why don't we cut her a break?'

It was Darrix.

The first boy turned and glared at him. 'She's a *half-demon!*' he said with a sneer.

Darrix just smiled and said in a quiet, friendly manner, 'So? I thought the way people acted made them bad, not what they looked like.' It was an accusation as well as a way of protecting her.

 By Dr Joseph Ireland "Dr Joe"

'Push off, Darrix,' the boy said, and shoved Darrix hard in the chest.

But Darrix didn't even move a length. He just kept smiling down at the boy, though there was a little threat under that smile now. For a moment the boy looked worried, while Darrix waited calmly, without moving.

Then the rude boy got even angrier. He threw her piece of paper on the floor. 'C'mon boys,' he said, 'this is *boring*.'

They walked out mumbling, and one of them pushed her again before he left. They kicked her paper too, but Darrix blocked it with a surprisingly swift movement of his feet. Before she could even move, he'd bent down and picked it up. He smoothed it out and looked at it.

'Oh!' he said, as if surprised that it really was letters. Still, he smiled, and then held it out to her. 'Don't worry about them,' he said. 'They'll grow up.'

She reached out and snatched the paper from his hands, almost angry that he'd had to help her out, but deep inside, grateful that he did.

'Thank you,' she muttered.

'You're welcome,' he said and, picking up his satchel, he went straight into class, whistling a happy tune.

The other boys didn't tease her as much from then on. It made her wonder. Darrix didn't seem to care what anyone else thought of him. How did someone get to be so confident?

***

The next day was Planasday: the day everybody had special

lessons that were supposed to prepare them for their natural role in life. The children of warriors went to battle training. The children of nobles went to law classes. The children of musicians spent the day practicing music. Most other students were celebrating, because they got to go home. The college was much emptier on Planasday, as one by one the parents and carers arrived to take students to their individualised work experience.

In the first few weeks they'd put her in the kitchens, but she hated the thought of turning the meat by hand again, almost as much as they seemed to fear the thought of her touching it. So, by the time the sun was well over the horizon once more no one had come to collect Kialessa.

The headmistress looked at her and breathed a long, tired sigh. 'Looks like you, dear, have yet again to be assigned into your place in this world,' she muttered.

Then she sighed again, her brow furrowed as though she was struggling to answer a question Kialessa had not asked. Eventually she spoke up again. 'I suppose you are free to wander the castle grounds as you see fit. Make sure you do not go far, as I may have reason to call you. Keep yourself out of mischief and trouble young girl, you hear? Don't want you wearing my trust any further.'

'Yes, honoured gentle,' Kialessa said with a polite curtsey. She hoped the headmistress had not heard anything to wear out her trust at all, but it could have been a dozen things; from the time she called a lord by the wrong title, and he'd threatened to have her tongue cut out, to the time she'd put the mops away incorrectly and they'd all fallen out, tripping a servant. Straightening out the folds of her only dress Kialessa slowly headed out.

She did not drag her feet, but she did not rush either. She felt sad. Why did no one want her? What was she to do? Her head was full of ideas and thoughts from another exhausting week of study, and all the excitement with the wizard. Perhaps she could just sit by the stream and rest? But it seemed a poor choice of activity. The other youth would be working hard. She was supposed to be working hard, too.

So she grabbed her papers: the ones Piex wrote out for her, the ones with the letters. There were so many to learn! Kialessa promised herself she'd practice every day and so she began pacing back and forwards, repeating aloud each letter and its sound one hundred times just like he'd told her to.

It became a soft, meditative mumble under her breath. Muttering her letters she found herself strolling along the many corridors and alleys of the small town that resided inside the castle's mighty walls. It was a huge place, full of a myriad of excellent hiding spots and places to sneak. *Really, it isn't very well defended from a spy*, she thought. An army might be hard pressed to take the gate with the well-armed guards and all, but it was no wonder that a single person had walked right up to the king's keep at night, when all the humans had hidden indoors, and helped himself to the king's saltshaker. He probably could have sat right down in the king's throne if he wanted! She wondered if they'd ever thought about that.

Yet as she wandered around the castle, guards shooing her from the occasional venue, she began to notice signs around the place. Little notices at every second door, sometimes great posters with words all over them. It soon became a game, and Kialessa would run from door to door trying to sound out new words. It was infinitely more fun than repeating letters a hundred times, and she felt she was learning more too. Door after door bore a message of one sort or another, and while she could do little more than sound most of them out, she was amazed at the words she knew once she heard them out loud.

And that was how she found someone she'd never expected to find indoors on Planasday. She couldn't believe her eyes. Why, when all the other students were out pursuing their future careers, did the early morning hours of Planasday find the mighty future warrior Darrix kneeling quietly at a religious shrine?

Isn't he a warrior? The younger brother of two respected warriors? she wondered. *Why is he not out studying battle, or at least mining like his dad?*

She waited there a moment, holding her breath by the wooden lintels of the little shrine, but he did not move. He was looking up at a great circle of wood, the symbol of a god she did not know, his lips moving but his voice silent.

What is he doing here?

She looked around. The high priestess was across the hall in a nearby room, and she smiled at Kialessa from behind a desk but kept working as though she didn't mind her being there at all. Apart from Darrix there was no one in the shrine. Perhaps she could talk to him?

Mustering all her courage, Kialessa tiptoed into the shrine. It was a simple room. There were several polished wooden pews for people to sit, and little candles along the walls and by the door. A wooden altar with a soft blue cushion on top rested at the centre of the far end of the room, underneath the great wooden circle towards which the young man prayed.

     By Dr Joseph Ireland "Dr Joe"

4 The prayerful warrior

'Darrix,' she whispered.

'Oh!' he said, so surprised he whacked his back on the pew behind him. Then he laughed. 'Oh, it's you Kialessa. Sorry, I didn't hear you come in. Please, sit down.'

She didn't.

'I hope you don't mind, gentle,' she said to him, using her most polite voice possible; the one her father used when he was speaking to people more important than he, which seemed to be everyone. 'I hope you don't mind, but I was wondering -'

'Gentle? I'm no gentle, Kialessa, I'm your same age.'

She smiled, and thought him polite to say so. 'Well, Darrix, I was wondering what you're doing.'

'I could ask you the same thing. Don't they have a job for you?' She did not answer and, sighing, he looked up at the large circle above the altar. 'I always come to the shrine all morning on Planasday. My father used to try to stop me, but I'd sneak out, and stay up late till I was no use the next day. Now he just lets me. I'm usually here till midday, when I go back to swordplay for the afternoon.'

'Yes,' said Kialessa, 'that's where I'd expect you.'

He smiled. 'I enjoy sword fighting, it's true, and wrestling, and archery.' He knelt back down on the cushions and put his palms together. 'But it's all empty unless I spend an hour here each morning.'

Kialessa didn't know what to think. *Every day*? She was surprised to learn he was so religious and devout. Then she begun to wonder what was fulfilling about looking up at an empty wooden symbol every day. She took a few steps closer to try to see what he saw.

'What is it?' she asked the young warrior.

'The Circle of the Eternal.'

'What's it for?' she said, getting closer.

'It's the symbol of my god,' he replied in a happy tone.

'Really?' she said. 'Which one?'

He laughed. He didn't seem uncomfortable at all about speaking his religious beliefs. Well, few did in their culture; priests were common enough. No one doubted the existence of the gods. Who could, when their devotees could imbue weapons with glowing light, or mould fire in their hands, or work miracles of healing and justice, and a thousand other prayers of power?

 By Dr Joseph Ireland "Dr Joe"

She'd been told in college that divine power was unlike magic, though they sometimes looked similar. The priest's power came as a gift from the gods, according to their immortal power and wisdom, rather than the imperfect attempts of mortal wizards who achieved their power from hours of study and memorisation of arcane science, language, and a whole lot of maths.

The first usefulness of the priests was in dedicating the works of humanity to the divine for protection and blessing – marriages, new roads, war and the like. The second was in council: interpreting dreams, telling the future and reading the signs the gods left in the world to warn people. The third was in calling down divine interventions, especially healing; every ruler had a number of priests of extraordinary faith for healing and protection. Rulers themselves were always devoted to one particular god or another, as were the people. She didn't know anyone who lacked a story of a long-lost relative who'd met a god sometime in the distant past, or just last week. Kialessa had always wondered what it would be like to meet a powerful god, but the gods had never seemed to notice her, and she had never felt the need to seek one out.

Yet there were thousands of gods to choose from: one for each season, even one for each day of the year. There were gods for every feeling or hope of the heart. There were even gods for the things they wanted to avoid, like death and sickness; gods that needed to be appeased to keep such terrible things away. She'd heard about them all in the stories back at the inn: Krigel, the mischief maker, who stole from the other gods; Pikal, the blade of justice, who punished those who crossed his path, and Math, the terrible god of nightmares.

But she'd never heard of this 'Eternal'.

'Is The Eternal a god of the old pantheon, or is he one of the gods of the non-human races?' she asked, trying to sound at least a little educated.

'Neither,' Darrix replied. 'He is a new god. Missionaries with dark skins from the northern countries brought his teachings to this land in my father's day. He never took to them, but they were always kind to me. When I first came to this college last year, I discovered King Dunnkan keeps a people's shrine to the Eternal, and ever since I've been coming whenever I can.'

'King Dunnkan worships The Eternal, too?' Kialessa asked, surprised.

'He does, at the royal shrine,' Darrix answered. 'This is the people's shrine. I can come here whenever I like.'

'Oh,' she wondered, 'and what is The Eternal a god of?'

'What do you mean?'

'You know, storms, fear, what not. Like Serros, the god of the sun or Lumos, his sister the moon?'

'He's not like the old gods.'

'What's he like, then?' Kialessa asked. She really wanted to know.

'He is the god of all things. Unlike the other gods, he is interested in us and loves us very much, and wants to help us, and have us help each other.'

'That's nice,' Kialessa smiled.

Darrix sat up on his heels, seeming eager to share his beliefs. 'He teaches us to show kindness, not only mercy, to our enemies. He teaches us to help those who take advantage of us. He teaches us to treat others the way we would want to be treated.'

'Pikal wouldn't like that,' Kialessa observed.

     By Dr Joseph Ireland "Dr Joe"

'No, he doesn't,' Darrix smiled, and then continued with a sad voice. 'You know, there's quite a bit of tension between the church of the old pantheon, and little churches like this one. We're lucky the king keeps a shrine. Most of them are vandalised eventually, even in Lenmer'el.'

'That's sad,' she admitted. 'But what's that big circle for?' She had moved quite close to it. She could see now that it was three rings, weaving about each other in a beautiful pattern. It was simple, but crafted with great care.

'The priestess tells me that the symbol was not given by The Eternal to us, but we created it to help us reach him. It can mean many things depending on what you need. Sometimes I see a light coming from inside.'

'Really?' Kialessa said.

'Yes, there was one just before you walked in. Not everyone can see the light, you know. Some say that the circle is a gateway; that angels and other messengers can come through to our world when the faith of those here is strong enough. Some say it is merely a symbol to represent to our minds greater things. Some … hey, what are you doing?'

Kialessa had hoisted herself up onto the little cushioned altar and was staring right through the circle, trying for all she was worth to see if there was a little light in there. She could see nothing but turned and jumped down when Darrix sounded so worried.

'I'm trying to see.' The words tumbled out of her so quickly they almost fell over each other.

He looked worried, but then laughed, and pointed at the altar. 'You're not supposed to put *yourself* on the altar!' He smiled and then added, 'well, not unless the priestess invites you.'

'Oh,' she said. 'I hope nothing happens!' She'd met priests who could scorch their enemies with divine fire. Divine, or profane …

'No, not with The Eternal,' Darrix explained, smiling. 'He's said to be very compassionate and eager to forgive.'

'That's nice,' she said with gratitude, but she took a few steps away to stand next to Darrix, just in case.

'What *do* you put on the altar?' she asked him.

'Injuries or sicknesses. People who are sick, I mean. Or sins. Often we use the altar to confess our sins privately or publicly to The Eternal, if we need to. We put our sins on the altar, giving them to The Eternal to heal. Or prayers, you can place your prayers on the altar.'

'Prayer?' she asked in disbelief. 'You mean, you actually *talk* to The Eternal?'

'Anyone can!' he laughed.

'Really?' she said. 'I thought you had to be worthy to talk to the gods.'

'Anyone can talk to The Eternal,' he explained.

But Kialessa was wary. Talking to gods could be *dangerous*. 'How?'

'Come,' he instructed, 'kneel here.'

She looked at him sideways. 'All right …' she said, eyeing him with caution. No one had ever invited her to kneel with them in prayer.

He smiled. 'Here's how it works. Sorry, here's how it works for me, when I pray. First, I speak His name. Then I express gratitude for things, even things that haven't gone well. Then I just talk to Him like He is really here. Like He's just sitting right next to me and listening to every word I say.'

'Just like that? Like another person or something?'

'Just like that,' he smiled.

'And you're not afraid he'll smite you for, I don't know, disrespect or something?'

Darrix just smiled. 'No, not with my God. He's said to be kind of like… a kind father who's interested in what I'm doing, rather than a demanding creator who requires obedience. I just talk to Him, or sometimes I let my mind wander in prayer. And I ask Him for the things I need.'

'Really? You pray for yourself?'

'Of course. I am a child of the Eternal too, so I'm my first responsibility. Anyway, when I am peaceful inside and it feels like time to finish, I close in the name of The Eternal. Then I just get up and do those things that make me feel happy. That's how I pray.'

There was a shuffle of feet, and the old dwarven priestess entered to set out a few new candles. Without looking at them she said, 'Very good Darrix, but there is one thing I would like to add: You don't need a formula, or a great circle, even a shrine to speak to The Eternal. He will hear any sincere prayer, in any manner, anywhere. There is great power in prayer, in the things that people sincerely believe. And when many people sincerely seek a certain thing with all their hearts, it truly is a kind of magic - it truly can create miracles.'

She nodded at them, leaving them to their thoughts and conversation.

Kialessa had never been taught how to pray. It sounded nice. Her parents kept a shine to Zhenshari, the blithling goddess of prosperity and trade, but they kept all the clay coins that travellers laid at her little bronze feet. That was as close to developing a relationship with a god that she'd ever known, or at least, that she could ever remember.

She looked up at the large, wooden circle and wondered what it would be like to feel as though someone godlike and powerful was watching over her, having a hand in her life, caring about what she became. In that thought, she imagined she saw a fleeting white light, like fire, radiating out from the circle, but in the next moment it was gone.

'What is it?' Darrix asked.

'Oh, nothing …' she said, just a little surprised.

He was quiet for a moment. 'Hey,' he said, 'would you like to pray with me?'

'Yeah, sure,' she replied. It was at least worth an attempt; he seemed to enjoy it enough. So, she knelt next to the older boy and put her hands like he showed her, and tried to pray.

She lasted less than two moments before she was sprawled out, sitting back comfortably on her heels, and hands in her lap. Darrix didn't seem to mind, he kept kneeling up without fidgeting, palms together, lips gently moving in prayer to a god she knew he'd never seen in person.

There was nothing else to do that day, so she let her mind wander in her prayer. She was thinking about her letters, about the classes she had to learn, about the cold little bed and undersized sheepskin that was all she had to keep her warm while she slept.

 By Dr Joseph Ireland "Dr Joe"

Suddenly she was *miserably* homesick. She wondered if she'd lost her mind and looked to see if Darrix had noticed. He was praying so hard it was no wonder she'd snuck up on him in the first place.

She had hated her home and yet, so far away, she discovered that there were things she missed about it. Things she missed terribly. She missed her warm place by the oven, with the soft straw she used to keep cosy. She missed the familiarity; she missed not having to think all the time!

But most of all she missed her family.

Even though when her mother spoke to her it was to order her around, Kialessa always knew she kept her fed and safe. Her father, often too drunk to stand, was so full of kind words and he always made sure she was inside at night.

She even missed annoying little Kiel and his worried attitude, and she wondered how he was doing. Perhaps she'd see him again when she went home for winter? Then she'd tell him all about the college, and about the king, and the people she'd met. Maybe she'd even teach him to read too! He'd like that. She'd always thought he could be something more than a dish washer. But it was she that had been given the chance to learn how to read, not him …

She missed them. So, in spite of herself, Kialessa shed a little tear for her family, far away, and wondered if they were thinking of her. Then she let her mind wander again, onto more pleasant things, and didn't really pay attention to her own thoughts or the time.

Finally, Darrix took a deep breath and looked up. 'Nice, isn't it?' She wondered what he meant, and then realised she did feel nice. She was surprised to find she had gone all peaceful and quiet inside. She felt … light, and watched her feelings in quiet wonder.

'I suppose we should be going now, midday and all,' Darrix said a moment later.

'What?' Kialessa said, disbelieving.

'Didn't you hear the bells?' he asked. 'It's lunch time.'

Kialessa was almost speechless in surprise. 'You're kidding.'

'I don't kid about *lunch*!' He smiled and then continued, a little more subdued. 'You know, Kialessa, no one's ever shared prayer with me before. Not one of my friends. They hardly ever even listen to what I believe!'

'Really?' Kialessa doubted him.

'It's true. They all take to the old gods. They don't understand The Eternal, and they're too afraid of offending other people to search out their own beliefs. So, thank you.'

'You're welcome,' she said. It made her smile to think that at least in one way, the most popular boy in college was sometimes all alone, and that she'd been lucky enough to get to know him. She liked what she had found out. If she had her way, she'd often be back to see him at this shrine.

Darrix was smiling too, but then he seemed to get concerned about something. He asked, 'Did you … I hope you don't mind me asking. Did you see anything?'

'Not really. The circle *might* have glowed white for a moment–'

'

'Didn't,' he stuttered, 'didn't you see the *fire?* It was all *over you*, the *whole time!*'

'Really?'

'Really. And I saw someone put their hands on your

shoulders at one point too. Heaven is really looking out for you, Kialessa.'

'Really?!' she didn't want to sound too hopeful, but she was. She had seen nothing, felt nothing. There was just some peace while she let her mind wander. Had there been someone or something to hold her while… she prayed?

'You, you didn't see any of that?' he said. He seemed sad.

She shook her head.

He sighed deeply and said, 'Just after I taught you how to pray the circle burst out the most brilliant light I've *ever* seen. I don't usually share this with others, not even the wizards can explain what I see.' He smiled sadly.

'It did shine a little just then,' she said. 'I thought I was imagining it. Perhaps this is just *your* gift.'

He smiled and laughed a gentle laugh. 'Do you think it's a gift? Some of the others would think me insane, or possessed. Sometimes … sometimes I can see this dark light around certain people, Kialessa. It frightens me.'

That made her nervous. Dark light? What was he talking about?

'But not you. I like being around you,' he said.

She felt like she could just faint right there and then; nobody had *ever* said they liked being around her.

She held his offered hand and struggled to her feet, surprised to find them quite numb from sitting.

'You know,' he pondered out loud, 'some of them tried to tell me that the Tae'anaryl can't pray. That they just can't hear the voice of the gods of good. I am glad to find out today that they were wrong.'

'As am I!' Kialessa said. Right then she was too happy to care about what anyone else thought, but she cared very much what he thought.

'Hey,' he asked suddenly, 'can I call you Kia?'

'Kia,' she laughed. So he'd given her a new name, a nickname just for her. It was a name others had used in disrespect, but from him …

'Sure, you can call me Kia. Kia it is,' she agreed smiling broadly, and then they went to lunch.

***

The next day was Serrosday, which meant the people were required by law to down tools and commit their time to religious devotion. Kia was dragged along again with the other girls to a tedious hour of droning devotionals and burnt cloth sacrifices to Serros, head god of the old pantheon, before she managed to escape for the shrine of The Eternal. There she found Darrix and thirty or so other people, dressed quite formally for some serious devotions. It looked as if it was going to be just as boring as Serros, but then the young and old split into groups and spent the rest of the morning discussing faith and good works and right and wrong. It was all very philosophical, and Kialessa found she loved it more than anything she'd learnt at the college. She chatted and pondered and debated along with the rest of them, which seemed to impress them very much.

Perhaps the best part of the day came in the afternoon, when she skipped lunch to sit by the loveliest duck pond she'd ever seen and do nothing more than look up at the sky. It was the most

 By Dr Joseph Ireland "Dr Joe"

peaceful day she'd ever known. There were no lessons to learn; no steaks to turn. Soon after, first Piex and then Darrix found her, and they all shared stories of magic and life and studies.

The next day, right in front of the whole class, Darrix dragged two of his buddies with him and sat right down beside her and Piex. They talked all during the midday meal about parents and gods and castles. The girls were speechless.

And Kialessa counted him her second friend.

The Chase

Sometimes we do stupid things. Sometimes those things result in changing the world! Other times, they are just stupid.
– Anon. cited in 'Recollections of the Tae'anaryl'

Kialessa was speechless. Everyone was speechless.

The soldier just stood there, glowering at the students, a wry smile playing on his lips as though daring one of them to challenge him. But who would, when he was the captain of the king's guard? He had almost as many medals of honour to his name as muscles under his chain-mail shirt, and that was sure to be matched by the number of weapons he carried around every day. He had countless axes, swords, and a dozen concealed daggers. He stood there, glaring at them, arms folded against his chest just to highlight his bulging arm muscles.

'My visit *should* be expected,' captain Bon Shur'e almost

shouted. 'I make it a tradition to check on each student at least once a year. I've been hearing some very good things about some of you. Some are saying the future of the king's guard might be in this very class, and I have come today to see if it's true. So today, we learn archery.'

No one said a thing, but Kialessa saw Darrix smile.

This is not the usual Lumday, Kialessa thought to herself. When it came to the king's college, Lumday, pronounced loom-day after the goddess of the moon, was just about everyone's favourite day. In the afternoon students would learn combat and weapon training. Books went down and swords came out, and often they would form small groups and join in mock battles. It was tough, vigorous, physical exercise after six hours of morning study.

But archery … they had never done archery before. In her first week Kialessa had been trained with a sword and soon found she was terrible at it. She didn't have the physical strength to use it properly and found it so hard to hold on to that anyone could knock it out of her hands. The next week the tutor let her choose her own weapon so, naturally, she'd gotten out her father's whip. After hours and hours of safety drills the tutor had told her she had a talent and she'd practiced with it as often as she could. Pretty soon the other students got the idea of giving her a whip's distance in combat training and in time it was she who was ripping weapons out of other people's hands.

But today's class was archery: archery, with a loud captain of the king's guard and two of the royal king's guard presumably just for show. The tutor was visibly sinking with nervousness and Kialessa began to wonder if he might disappear into his boots altogether.

She wasn't feeling so good either. She had never even held a bow, let alone fired one.

'Right, get the bows!' the captain roared.

'But, sir, we haven't had time to cover the usual safety train-' the tutor muttered.

'Forget that. Safety is for fools and wizards. Let'm learn from *experience*! That's what I say! Wounds *heal*, boy. Now, ***get the bows***!'

Everyone scurried to comply. The captain was clearly the kind of person used to having people obey orders without question.

'He ought not speak so unkindly of wizards,' Piex muttered with a sigh. 'I suppose I shall have to endure this training yet further. The time could be better spent in study. You know, I've already finished reading every book the wizard gave me, and he's given me some more. *Reticulon's Nefarious Incantations –*'

'Oh come on, Piex,' Darrix interrupted. His two other good friends were standing near and testing their bow strings. 'Even apprentice wizards need to learn how to use a bow.'

'Learn I must, but I fear I shall never learn it well,' he muttered in reply.

'Less talk, more action! Take aim!' the captain roared, grinning. Less than half the students seemed ready and brief chaos ensued as they all scurried to line up.

The captain continued his thunderous speech. 'Goblins and troll scum rarely give the time you students seem to need. Come now, my two soldiers here would have put out a dozen eyes by the time you let loose your first arrows. Magic is impressive, but no troll shaman will cause you grief with an arrow in his throat!

Line up, line up young soldiers!!'

The tutor shuffled over to give Kialessa and another newer student the basics of using a bow, but the captain was impatient. 'Fire at will!' he ordered.

The other students let loose a random flurry of arrows, most not even hitting the targets twenty paces away. They reloaded frantically, trying to impress the captain, or at least not catch his ire.

Kialessa watched Darrix while the students fired and the tutor talked to her, his words not making much sense at all. But Darrix stood up tall, holding his bow string steady, a determined look of concentration etched onto his young face. Unlike the others, firing at random, he seemed to be waiting.

The tutor noticed her watching and stopped talking. 'Why does he wait?' she asked him.

'Perhaps he is waiting for the wind? Or he just enjoys making us all watch? Or perhaps he is waiting for the moment, the mystical combination of air and earth, of bow and bowman, when time and energy coalesce into a perfect moment of – Ho, what luck! Good shot, Darrix!'

Now that was poetic, Kialessa thought, and Darrix had just hit a bullseye on the nearest target.

'Harrah! That's the spirit. One less goblin eye to worry about!' the captain bellowed.

'You see, Kia, it's very easy,' Darrix said. 'You do it!'

'Oh no, not today. I need to watch!'

'Go on!' he grinned with encouragement, pushing his bow into her hands. The captain smiled and even Piex agreed she should give it a go. The whole class stopped to watch.

She felt a little nervous, but decided she couldn't make too much of a fool of herself. She took aim, but her first arrow slipped from her grasp and clattered to the ground. The students all laughed.

'Hey,' Darrix called. They stopped their sniggering.

The tutor ignored the bickering and focused on helping another young girl to hold her bow. At the king's college, students were supposed to learn life's lessons. They had to sort out their own troubles without much interference from the tutors, unless it got violent. It was considered part of helping them prepare for the 'real world'.

Kialessa didn't really like that rule.

'Try again,' the captain ordered, his voice soft for once. Kialessa sighed. At least she would get one arrow off today!

She fired, and off it went, skirting the very edge of the target and flinging upwards at a sharp angle so that it went high into the air; air that was blowing back her way. Students squealed and dashed to get out of the way. One of them nearly got hit on the head and shouted in protest. The captain burst out laughing. Kialessa looked at their angry faces. *How rude,* she thought. *No one was hurt, and it is only a practice arrow.*

Some of them mumbled some very unkind things, but she wasn't going to let herself get angry, she was going to keep practicing till she got a bullseye and then they wouldn't laugh any more.

She pulled the bow string and held it a long, long time. She waited till everyone fell silent. She felt the wind and touched the earth that connected her to the target. In her mind she saw the arrow fly right into the centre of that target, and she waited for *the moment.*

     By Dr Joseph Ireland "Dr Joe"

Suddenly, it was very quiet inside, her feelings were very calm. *So, this must be the moment,* she thought.

She let the arrow fly, and it landed right next to the centre of the bullseye.

'See, you can do it!' Darrix said.

'Truly serendipitous!' Piex said. Kialessa had no idea what that meant but it sounded positive.

The captain looked surprised, but everyone else muttered about beginner's luck. However, five moments later, by the time she'd shot out her third bullseye off only ten arrows, people weren't laughing any more. They were all very silent. It seemed Kialessa was a natural at this, too.

'Hmm. What'd you say to her?' the captain asked the tutor.

'I told her about *the moment,*' he replied in wonder.

'What's that?'

'I don't know, I just made it up,' the tutor confessed.

The captain then ordered them out to collect their arrows and started coaching each student individually while his royal guards waited at attention. A few moments later Kialessa was lining up her next shot when she heard a voice.

'Hey, Kialessa!' the rude boy shouted. It was the one who'd stolen her paper away a week or two ago. 'Why don't you try your **beginner's luck** on the far target!'

Everyone agreed.

It was very far away.

But she was more than happy to show up the rude boy, so she took aim. It took a little longer to find the moment, but she did and let her arrow fly. It was dead true, and right on track to hit the centre ring if not the bullseye, when all of a sudden the target fell down. Her arrow skittered off the top edge and went flying away into the distant woods.

The rude boy had tied a string to it and pulled it down. He laughed at her for all he was worth, and so did his friends.

'Ha, ha, missed that one!' he jeered.

Kialessa was incensed. The captain and tutor seemed busy with other things. She snapped. *How could he be so rude?* Her face went hot, and she clenched her fists in anger.

'You cheated!' she shouted and stalked right up to him.

'Oooh, so angry!' he teased, hiding behind his friends. 'What ya gonna do demon girl, fry me with your evil eyes?'

It was a terrible insult. She raised her hand and jumped forward to slap him, but then she heard the captain's voice call out.

'You two, halt!'

Kialessa and the rude boy both apologised without hesitation. It was a terrible thing to hit another student at the college outside combat training. At least, there was a rule for that.

But there is plenty of combat training, she smiled to herself.

'What all this about?' the captain's voice grumbled with threat.

'Sir, he tipped over the target after challenging Kialessa to hit it,' Darrix explained, showing him the string.

'Cheating …' the captain's voice trembled with anger. 'You boy, back to the college. Your father will hear of this!'

The lad rushed away, tears streaming from his eyes. Kialessa didn't dare look up at the captain. Getting in trouble was not something she wanted to do today, or any day, though it usually happened at least twice.

'Ah, sir,' one of the rude boy's friends said, 'who's going to get the arrow?'

'What? Oh, tae'anaryn, you get it.'

She had too much sense to protest that, and hurried off to find the arrow that had flown so far that now it was lost somewhere in the nearby woods. Darrix asked permission to go with her, and Piex joined in anyway. For a while they just walked in silence while the other students had the privilege of watching the captain shooting anything he wanted to. His aim was amazing, though his enchanted bow *Hera Lira* no doubt helped.

'Don't let that boy's bullying bother you,' Darrix said, after a while. 'He'll grow up.'

'Not if I beat him senseless first,' she said through her clenched, pointed teeth. 'Oh, how he makes me mad! Why does he treat me like that?'

Piex answered, 'I think it may be because he fears your race and seeks to establish his own poor social standing by being seen as superior to someone such as yourself.'

'You mean he tries to make himself feel big by making me feel small?' she translated.

'Yes, that is correct.'

'Fool,' she muttered.

'Well, I just think he likes you,' Darrix said.

'What?' Kialessa couldn't believe he'd suggested that.

'Some people do that. They don't know how to act around someone they like and so they become very silly.'

'That's *crazy*!' Kialessa argued.

'Yes, but true!' he laughed.

'What, so I'm supposed to *thank* him because he's trying to say he likes me?' she asked.

'Well, no. Bullying is still wrong.' Darrix agreed.

'So,' she pondered, 'either he's a bully because he hates me …'

'No,' Piex corrected, 'fears you.'

'Or he's a bully because he likes me?' Kialessa said.

Darrix laughed, 'pretty much sums it up!'

'So how do I deal with it?' she muttered to herself.

'Well, I'm sure Darrix and I can agree on one thing,' Piex mused, 'some enemies are best simply ignored. He is not worthy of your attention, Kialessa. Giving him attention when he's rude contributes to the negativity of the situation.'

She couldn't see his point, yet wasn't saying something a way of dealing with bullies?

'He has a point,' Darrix said. 'Ignore him unless he has something sensible to say, and treat him with dignity when he does. Then, one day when he grows up, he will give you dignity in return. Reward the kind of behaviour you like by giving him your attention, since it is what he seems to want.' Once more Darrix sounded very grownup.

'Where'd you learn all that?'

He didn't really answer her question, but said, 'There is a scripture that teaches "the wicked are their own punishment", and we saw that in action today. His own actions got him in trouble. But then you almost hit him, which would have been twice as bad, and then you would be sharing his punishment, or worse.'

Probably worse, Kialessa thought. She was glad she'd decided to listen when the captain called out.

 By Dr Joseph Ireland "Dr Joe"

They made her think. *If he won't listen when I tell him I don't like it, then I ignore deliberate provoking. Reward decent behaviour.* At least it was something. Perhaps she could influence a bully's actions towards her. All without slapping him in the face.

She thought about it till they'd reached the edge of the field and began to scout around. There was a bit of disagreement among them about where and how far the arrow had gone so they went in three different directions to look for it, scrounging around in the underbrush. They searched for a good ten moments, getting further and further away from each other. Kialessa was just looking through some bushes, the college group so far away she could no longer hear them, when she looked up.

There, standing on a branch high up in the tree, was a figure cloaked in grey.

She gasped in surprise and threw herself against the tree trunk so that he could not see her. Almost too frightened to breathe she peeked out and looked up. Without a doubt it had to be the intruder. He was *back*.

He wore the same grey cloak as before, and was looking out towards the castle with some kind of peep object, a scope of some sort. He watched unmoving, and would have been impossible to see from anywhere except from right under that tree.

She looked about for the others, hoping to find a friend. But Piex was nowhere to be seen, and Darrix was too busy looking for a silly arrow see her frantic gestures. She was too afraid to call out to him. Perhaps, if she waited long enough, the intruder would come down and she could get a look at his face? Then she'd tell the captain, and they would find him, and find out what he was trying to do, and why he was trying to poison Lenmer'el's king.

Suddenly there was a rustling of branches as Piex stumbled through the brushes nearby.

'Here you go Kialessa,' he stuttered, 'I found your–'

But he didn't finish the sentence because she shoved her hand over his mouth. His dragon pupils dilated in fear and his skin went white with fright. She pointed up at the intruder.

Piex spotted him straight away. 'Who is he?' he whispered.

'The intruder,' she replied. 'If we wait, we might see who it is.'

'Intruder? What intruder?' He asked with such a quiet voice she almost couldn't hear him.

So no one had told them about the intruder? That was probably a mistake. How could they catch a person no one knew about?

A moment later Darrix snuck up. He'd seen the pointing and looked at them like he wanted to know what was happening.

'Who's that?' His voice was soft against the tree trunk.

'Not sure,' she replied, 'but I saw him before trying to put poison in the king's salt.'

'Poison!' Piex exclaimed, just a little too loud.

The intruder gasped, and looked down. Then, from the depths of his hood, Kialessa could see him smile. With a movement so swift it was almost inhuman, he swept his scope into his cloak and swung off the branch. Running from branch to branch, he began to leap away from them and deeper into the forest.

'After him!' Kialessa shrieked.

He was so fast. In a moment, he swept down to the ground and taunted them with mischievous laughter.

Piex soon fell behind; the last she heard of him was a loud protest about how foolish it all was. Darrix ran first, thrusting the branches aside with great skill. But then the intruder slid down a moss-covered log on a steep incline and Darrix drew up short.

'Better let him –' he began.

But Kialessa waited for nothing and slid right down after him.

'Wait, Kia, it's too dangerous!' Darrix shouted.

She was determined not to let the intruder escape her this time. He threatened the king, and the kingdom. And that meant everyone she cared about, even herself.

She chased him like a wolf racing after its prey, but he was enjoying the chase. Her breath was ragged, but he still had air enough to laugh.

Suddenly she came to a steep ravine. The only way to cross was a thin branch. He stood there, his grey cloak rustling in the afternoon breeze, daring her on.

She took a faltering step on the branch. It sunk under her feet but did not give way.

Hey, she told herself. *It's just like walking along the fence. The ground is just a few steps away.*

With growing courage, she sped along the branch. 'I'm coming to get you!' she shouted.

He laughed. He could have broken the branch and sent her crashing into the valley below, but he did not. He just laughed again until she was almost in arm's reach; could almost smell his warm breath.

Then he ran.

He was much faster this time, and she soon realised how tired she was. She couldn't seem to get enough air but, mustering all her will, she began to close the gap once more. It hadn't even crossed her mind what she would do if she ever caught him.

Suddenly he stopped at the far edge of a clearing. He seemed to be waiting.

With great care, keeping her eyes everywhere, she began to walk up to him. There was something suspicious about his calm manner. Without any warning two great branches sprang towards her. It was a trap! With a squeal she leapt up off her feet, twisted in the air, and landed in a rough heap on the ground. Before he had a chance to move, she got back on her feet and leapt towards him.

And… that was when he ran straight up.

She'd never seen anyone do that before. He ran upwards, up a tree, like it was a floor. He was well and truly out of her reach in less than a second.

'Who are you?!' she demanded in frustration, struggling to catch her breath. 'Why are you trying to harm my king?'

He just laughed. It was a dark, smooth laugh that Kialessa knew she'd heard from somewhere before.

Then she had an idea. If she couldn't catch him, maybe she could shoot him with the practice arrow Piex had found. It was blunt, but it flew well, and if he was an enemy to the king …

'Come down now and deliver yourself to the king,' she warned him, 'or I'll shoot you.'

It was incredibly brave, or foolish. Then he spoke, and his voice sounded so familiar, and yet she couldn't for the life of her tell where she'd heard it. 'That's very courageous of you, young tae'anaryn.' His voice was smooth and insulting, and just *so familiar*. 'I admire your courage.'

'Who *are* you?' she demanded.

He laughed again. 'You cannot catch me. You never will,' he teased. 'Others have tried; they never have. So go back to your classes, child. Tell them all about the grey shadow you found spying on the king once more. You know, you continue to cause me a great deal of inconvenience.'

'What are you doing here!?' she insisted. She aimed the arrow right at his heart.

'You have no idea what's coming to your world,' he whispered.

She had no intention of finding out what evil he intended for her or any in her world, so she took aim. It was easier than before, even though the target was further and smaller. It was the chase, and the silence among the trees. She found the moment. It was a perfect shot that flew straight to his heart.

Yet, with a movement so swift she couldn't even see it he knocked the arrow right out of thin air with a curved knife she didn't know he had. The broken pieces cluttered to her feet.

'Goodbye, little one, it is destined that we meet again!'

He disappeared into the shadows, his laughter echoing so

5 Right out of the air

perfectly around the clearing and into the dark woods that she had no idea where he went. For a moment she just stood there, struggling to regain her breath in the darkness.

Silence.

Kialessa had not noticed how very dark it was in this part of the forest, where she had never been before: dark, unfamiliar and frightening.

Kialessa heard a twig snap behind her in the forest and drew her breath sharply. With a falling pit in her stomach, she realised that she had just shot off her only weapon. She clutched the bow in two hands and wielded it like a clumsy club. Eyes red with fear she cringed back against a tree. Perhaps it was a wolf, or a wild posk, or a drake?

She did not feel so brave any more.

As she watched, a dark shadow stood up among the trees. It was tall, at least her height. She almost screamed as the shadow stepped into the clearing.

It was Darrix.

'Kia, how glad I am I found you!' he said.

'Not as glad as I am. Come on, let's get out of here.'

'Did you catch him?' he asked. He seemed ready to believe she had.

'Not today,' she replied, and they went back to tell the others.

***

The captain, of course, was livid. 'Have you no idea just how much danger you placed yourselves in, children? You are not heroes or guards of the king's palace to go chasing bandits and assassins into the forest! You're lucky you didn't get your throat cut out, girl! Why didn't you run to tell me as soon as you saw him?'

Piex burst into tears as soon as the shouting started and protested it wasn't his fault and he only chased the bandit

 By Dr Joseph Ireland "Dr Joe"

because the others did, and he didn't get very far anyway. Darrix was too obedient to disagree and stood like a soldier on trial.

'I'm not sure we did the right thing,' he told her later.

But Kialessa was angry. The intruder had already escaped them once before. Clearly the captain didn't have his priorities straight.

'I never, never want to hear of you chasing after criminals again, do you hear?' he insisted.

When Kialessa replied, it was in a whisper almost too soft to hear, 'I will stand up to any who threatens my king and this kingdom.'

He gave a wry smile, and nodded his acknowledgement of her wish. 'Detention, the rest of the day,' he told her anyway.

She served it gladly.

The Enchantress

I thought my life was ruined: I was betrayed! I was forsaken by the gods! Then I began to see how this disaster could be an opportunity, a blessing in disguise. That was when I truly became powerful. That was when I truly became free.

– Py Gedzelai; tutor, Studies of Athletics and Physical Prowess

Winter had ended, the late frost just a memory on the grass each dawn. Kialessa loved to wake up early to try to catch a glimpse of the frost fairies out doing their job fighting back the spring. It was a job they never won, which was a good thing. It meant that things would change.

For two more weeks Kialessa looked for the intruder every night, but he was nowhere to be seen. Piex was adamant that she give up the search, but still she would sneak out late at night just in case she was the only one destined to find him. Kialessa was glad the guards never arrested her and just sent her on, but soon she got so good at hiding they never saw her at all. After a while it looked like the intruder was not coming back, at least, not for now.

The days soon became routine. Kialessa was up before dawn just like all the other students, washing her face and hands, readying her books and hair. They studied indoors all morning with one class or another, and always with different students: language, history, arithmetic or heraldry. The lunch hour was everyone's favourite time. They all finished well before the tutors and so had a good chance to do their own thing for a while. Much to everyone's relief the afternoons were usually devoted to more physical classes: combat training, care for beasts, armoury and the like. It kept her from going crazy with continual bookwork and all the other students, with perhaps the exception of Piex, were grateful.

With Piex and Darrix to help her, Kialessa found she could understand a lot more than she thought she could. The classes were varied and interesting. She never complained, like many of the nobles' children, that any of the classes were unnecessary or boring. Everything was new. And now that she had two friends: one who taught her to read every lunch time, and another whose friendship protected her from almost all the bullying. Kialessa was very happy.

And then *she* turned up.

Her name was Allastassia. She was only a year older than Kialessa but dressed like an adult. She was part dryad, daughter of a half dryad. Kialessa found herself envious of the older girl, who always seemed so confident and social. Much to Kialessa's disgust all the boys took to drooling over her right away, and the girls flocked to her like she was royalty. She looked like it, too:

tall, confident and pretty. She had the biggest sea blue eyes Kialessa had seen, with long curls of auburn hair that were never, ever out of place, and that changed colours with the seasons. This season, being spring, Allastassia's hair sprouted random flowers. Seriously, *flowers!*

Allastassia owned more outfits than most people had fingers, and her rich family were always buying rare and interesting items like mysterious trinkets from faraway lands or powerful magical items from across the world. Her whole family were high ranking nobles in King Dunnkan's court and had just returned from a diplomatic mission overseas. The other girls all stayed up late just to hear her tell her stories.

It was ridiculous.

Yet even the tutors were in love with Allastassia. They loved to ask her questions to hear her witty and polite replies. It annoyed Kialessa no end. How could they be so preferential to someone just because they had long wavy hair and sea blue eyes?

It might still have been all right, but it took Allastassia about three seconds to work out that Kialessa was the one *everyone* was supposed to hate. So the pretty girl began a campaign to humiliate her at every turn. She would ask the most innocent sounding questions only to turn it into an insult, and everyone would be laughing at Kialessa once more. She even had the audacity to do it in front of certain tutors, who seemed to know no better than to laugh along.

Allastassia even tried to steal her friends from her.

'Come on, Kia,' Piex said, when she finally brought up the fact he wasn't helping her learn how to read much anymore. 'You're being jealous. She's not so bad.'

6 The enchantress

'That's just because she hasn't started picking on you,' Kialessa retorted. 'Then you'll see what I mean. She can make everyone your enemy without even trying! And she's the kind of bully you just can't ignore. Believe me, I've tried!'

But what really hurt Kialessa was that Darrix didn't hang around them so much; Allastassia had seen to that. Darrix had often tried to stop to chat for lunch, but she was all over him. It wasn't because she liked him, Kia thought with anger, but because he was the most popular boy in college. She gathered all the most popular people in college around her like flies to ointment.

So Kialessa and Piex were all alone once more, while Allastassia impressed everyone with her wit and charm. She was doing it now, orchestrating the girls in some kind of dancing she'd learnt from a foreign land, much to the interest of everyone else. Kialessa and Piex were sitting on the steps, Kialessa pretending to form her letters into words so that she could write her long promised letter to the king. Piex was reading another book the wizard had given him, as he did late into every night. Wizards were rare and the chance to study with one was even rarer. Piex had been given a wonderful opportunity, and with Allastassia's distractions he had even less time for friendship now.

But the thing that really impressed everyone the most was that Allastassia was an enchantress, the daughter of an enchantress. Not one in a thousand people had the enchanter's talent.

Kialessa turned to ask Piex, 'What is an enchantress?'

'Hmm. How to explain that in simple terms … Well, the world is full of magic, magic made up of the thoughts and desires of living beings. See, for wizards, magic is a science, with strict rules and formulas to understanding. We strive to uncover the words and ideas that represent the pure forms of creation, bound together in the powerful language of dragons, created by the gods at the beginning of time. Yet, for the enchanters, magic is all an art. They just … insist … that things happen. Appalling, really. They don't study at all! Not like us wizards. Wizards have to work very hard,' he said, and went back to reading his book.

He can concentrate anywhere, thought Kialessa with gnawing

     By Dr Joseph Ireland "Dr Joe"

envy. It was getting harder and harder for her to concentrate at the college knowing that at any hour Allastassia would have them all laughing at her once more.

In that, she was right.

The next class was Studies of Athletics and Physical Prowess. They were learning how to keep fit, to run and balance and climb. Kialessa loved the class and its tutor. He wasn't human, but an old outcast from his own people: a Gedzelai. His skin was grey, and stretched strangely over his face so that his nose looked crooked and broken. He was old, too, even by Gedzelai standards. But just like all the Ged, as they were called locally, he was exceptionally skilled at unarmed combat. He could run on a rope, or climb up a stone wall as if it was a ladder. She'd seen him catch swords in his bare hands or fall from great heights without hurting himself, even though he was quite old.

Today he'd set up an obstacle course. They had to make their way across a thick board over which he moved a dozen ropes like snakes. They were not supposed to touch those ropes. Beneath them a pile of cushions represented lava they were supposed to avoid.

Today, all of them were falling in the lava.

He chuckled. 'Children, this game teaches us many things worth knowing in life. See the plank as an analogy for the journey you must take. It is often strewn with snakes you must avoid, and to fall off is death. However, if you will look, you will see there are many places you may stand safely.'

He was always quoting the teachings of wise masters or looking for deeper meanings in mundane things, and he spoke in a strange accent, in which he often mistook one letter for another. 'And that is why you will all try again,' he said. 'Come, Kialessa, you are fleet of foot. Take the journey.'

'Oh, I hope she doesn't trip on her tail,' Allastassia jeered. She sounded worried, but her eyes held meanness and the whole class laughed.

Kialessa turned brown with shame and hurt, and hid her face.

Allastassia had done it again.

Then the tutor did something he wasn't supposed to do. Students at the college were supposed to sort out their own problems. They were supposed to deal with bullying in their own time. But he walked right up to Allastassia, and looked down at her with anger in his eyes.

'No one is to mock another student in my class,' he whispered. His voice was soft, yet so very angry. She turned red and looked down at her feet. 'Am I to be mocked,' he said, 'because my skin is not pink or my people not yours?'

'No, sire,' Allastassia whispered, trembling. No one dared to make a sound.

'Come, Kialessa,' he said in his soft voice and began to walk away.

Where is he going? Kialessa wondered and hurried up to his side. He walked right into the equipment storage room, which seemed an odd thing to do, and then shut the door on the quiet and curious class.

'That pink girl does have a point though,' he said. 'You *are* tripping over your tail.'

Kialessa looked down, feeling very sorry for herself once more. 'It always gets in the way,' she muttered.

He was silent for a moment and then put a kind hand on her shoulder.

'Perhaps that's because you're *treating* it that way.'

She looked up, not understanding what he meant.

'Everything in life is an opportunity,' he said, 'even if it is a dangerous opportunity. For instance, to one of those children to have a tail such as yours might be an obstacle, but to you it is a part of your strength. It is a part of what you are and what makes you unique. Try to see it as an opportunity. Other children might not understand that, but you do not have to think like other children. You can think like yourself.'

She stared at her tail then, peering out from under her pretty dress. It was long and thin, and very curvy. She could hold things with it, and probably used to when she was little. But it had made others seem uncomfortable and so she'd learned to hide it, curling it into a spiral in her lower back. How could it be an opportunity?

'You must learn to use every advantage you have,' her Gedzelai tutor answered her questioning look. 'Not only your wits, your strength, and your skill, but also your horns, your tail, and your skin which does not burn. All other students will use the gifts they have. Humans, for instance, make many friends, and seem to be able to survive just about anywhere. If you are to fulfil your destiny and find the greater happiness, you must also use every gift you have. To do that you must embrace *everything* that comes at you in life as an *opportunity*.'

She wondered how she might do that, peering at the little dusk red tail she kept hidden underneath her dress. The tail that she kept wrapped around her legs in class so that it didn't accidentally pop out. The tail she kept hidden when she bathed.

'Come,' he said, rifling through a closet, 'put this on.'

It was a pair of shorts.

Kia couldn't believe it. Only the boys were supposed to wear shorts in studies of athletics and physical prowess! Although the female soldiers wore trousers just as the men, as did the athletes and many of the circus performers, in this class only the boys wore shorts.

She looked at him, pleading that he wouldn't ask her to break another rule at the college.

He gave her an understanding smile. 'This policy of making girls wear dresses in my class has always bothered me, and now I cannot allow you to be prevented from reaching your potential by a silly dress code. Kialessa, trust me. There is *no shame* inherent in your nature, so you need to release your tail so that you can learn to use it properly, as an opportunity and a tool, and not an obstacle. That is how it was meant to be.'

She didn't know what to do, but in the end she reasoned that most of the other students didn't like her anyway so what did she have to lose? So, after he left, she took off her dress and put on shorts and a thin shirt. Then she re-tied her hair into a tight ponytail on the back of her head.

He must have threatened the other students to make no mean comments when she returned. He must have done a very good job because she could not hear a sound when she came out. They didn't even dare snicker, though she feared they were scandalised at the sight of her in shorts, and just held in their cruellest laughter.

They'd never seen her tail in full before. It was long, and reached down below her feet. She could scratch her head with it if she wanted to. As she walked, Kialessa realised that her tail was made to stand upright, even though she'd kept it pointed down and hidden under her dress her whole life. It waved and flicked around in great anticipation, as though it was happy. Then a great smile lit Kialessa's face as she found herself happy to be herself: a tae'anaryn with a tail and not one bit ashamed.

'Now,' her tutor said and smiled. 'Kialessa, cross the boards.'

At first, she was anxious once more, and gulped down hard. *How will I even make it past the first rope?* But as she dodged and weaved, skipped and hopped, she was amazed to find she made it past the first six ropes quite easily. She was equal best to any other student in their group. Darrix had made five and Piex, only one!

She marvelled at her tail. It seemed it was designed to help her keep her balance in ways she'd never even realised! This was a new trick she promised herself she'd remember.

The latter ropes were more difficult; they thrashed more than ever. *If only I can make just one, I will break the class record!*

Yet, somehow, her first step went wrong. Instead of standing on the board she stood right on a rope, and in her hurry to leap off it she lost her footing. She fell down. Without thinking, she wrapped her tail around the beam and gripped on with all her strength. She fell sideways but did not hit the cushions that were the lava. Instead, she swung around and clutched the underside of the board. It tilted dangerously sideways, but she did not fall off.

The class gasped.

'Keep moving!' her tutor shouted. 'Get back up each time you fall.'

But that was when Kialessa discovered that it's very hard to climb back on a board when you're upside down. She scratched with her nails, but couldn't seem to get the leverage she needed.

'Use your tail!' Darrix suddenly shouted. It was common for students to shout encouragement at each other, but none had ever cheered for her. They cheered that she might fall off. With his example, another student and then two, cheered her on.

I will not let them down.

She wrapped her tail around the board as far as it would go, and clutched and clawed with her legs and hands. She gradually managed to get back on top.

About half the class cheered.

Her courage soared. Leaping and dancing among the twisting ropes she sprang along the board. There were six, then five. Piex and Darrix ran to the other side, screaming her on, waiting to greet her there. Four ropes, then three. Other students joined them, and they were cheering and chanting her name. Two ropes, then one…

…She had made it. She threw herself into their arms and they cheered and cheered and cheered.

'You did it,' Darrix boasted. 'You just smashed the class record!'

'Likely the college record for attempts made on the first day, too,' Piex added.

Many students patted her on the back. Most of them were impressed. Some of them might have even wished they had something as useful as a tail too.

'Enough!' her tutor suddenly shouted in a very loud voice. It silenced the class. 'So, child, you have mastered the writhing ropes? Then I give you a task I usually defer to the older students.' He shouted words of arcane power. *'Funis; vivo!'*

In the next moment the ropes no longer twisted along the

ground; they magically stood up in the air. Many of them swung in wild loops of their own accord. They whipped and flailed in random patterns as high as her head. But two others reared up like snakes. They twisted and writhed as though they were alive and hungry, threatening her with cloven tongues of thread.

The whole class oohed in wonder.

'Come, Kialessa,' the tutor ordered, standing at the far end of the plank. 'Be the first to face the senior students' challenge!'

She stood up on the board. *This is madness. Surely no one could make it through such a magically writhing mess?* Yet perhaps there was some pattern to it all, an … opportunity?

She looked closely. She realised that the ropes followed a pattern, with only two of them serving as living snakes. Each sixth rope formed a sphere through which only the snakes could enter. If she could jump inside that sphere and keep skipping, ignoring the other ropes and fending off the snakes, then perhaps she could make the far end after all?

She waited till the right moment and leapt in, hopping from one foot to another while the rope spun around her. The twisting sphere slowly began working its way from one end of the plank to the other. She laughed. Although the ropes flailed around widely, none of them could touch her.

None except the two snakes …

Sure enough, they darted in one at a time to try to push her off the plank, or to wrap themselves along her limbs if they could. To avoid them, Kialessa danced and skipped from one foot to another. She had nothing to defend herself with and had to dodge, jump and twirl, and all the time hop, hop, hop.

She lost track of time, giddy with enthusiasm for a genuine

challenge. But, when she saw the platform that was the end of the task just a few paces away, she let her concentration slip for half an instant. She was too impatient, too ready to leap right on, and the snakes took their opportunity. Before she could think they'd managed to wrap themselves around her arms and they threw her bodily onto the cushions on the floor. Kialessa squealed in surprise and dismay.

But the whole class cheered. Piex and Darrix ran up to her and patted her on the back.

'Your ability is exceptional!' Piex said with a cheer.

'You almost completed the senior students' challenge!' Darrix thumped her on the shoulder in congratulations.

'Well done,' the tutor said, as his ropes sunk to the floor. 'You have done far better than any previous student at this college.'

'Thank you,' she panted, 'for believing in me.'

'Young girl,' he smiled, 'it was only your failure to believe in yourself that was holding you back.'

She smiled. Everyone smiled.

Everyone, that is, except a tall auburn dryad girl with flowers sprouting from her pretty, perfect hair, looking at her with daggers in her eyes.

***

It was late that night when they attacked her. They must have been planning it all day. One of them had gone out to distract the headmistress while the other girls, four of them, held Kialessa's arms and legs to her bed before she had the chance to even wake up.

          By Dr Joseph Ireland "Dr Joe"

By the time she did they already had her securely held.

Kialessa screamed. 'What are you doing?'

'Be quiet, demon,' a cold voice said. It was Allastassia. 'The headmistress is busy now, and you don't want to wake up the other students, do you?'

She spoke in a sweet and dangerous voice, as though it was all a game. But Kialessa knew that all the other students would already be wide awake, and were all too frightened to do anything. 'I know how to deal with your kind,' she cursed in a mean voice, and sat right down on Kialessa's chest, pinning her to her bed.

Kialessa was terrified. What was she about to do?

'My uncle was killed by an evil demon, just like you,' Allastassia sneered. 'I don't like you Kia, and I'm going to show everyone just how *evil* you are. It's not enough that you magicked that tutor into telling me off, and then used your infernal sorcery to steal my boyfriend.'

'Boyfriend?'

'Don't play stupid with me,' she said.

Kialessa wondered who she meant. Then she realised: Darrix. He'd stayed by her and Piex for dinner, not Allastassia.

'Darrix is not your boyfriend,' she said. 'He has his own choice –'

'Don't be stupid, demon! He is as good as mine and everyone, except you, already knows that. But I'm going to show him that you're evil and after that nice boys like Darrix will stay well away from you.'

She reached for something in her nightdress.

Kialessa struggled against the girls that held her arms, but they held on for dear life.

'Struggle and I'll scratch you,' one of them threatened.

But, underneath their bravery, Kialessa could tell they were afraid. What did they fear about her? Or were they afraid of Allastassia?

'I have a little enchantment my mother taught me.' She smiled in triumph. 'It burns the mark of a holy god into the flesh of evil creatures, even those immune to normal flames. It's quite tricky. It's taken over a year for me to master it. Now I'm going to burn this holy mark into your forehead so that everyone will know just how evil you are!'

'I'm not evil!' Kialessa shouted.

The young enchantress pulled out a large symbol that fit into the palm of her hand. It was a beautiful platinum circle embossed with delicate leaf patterns. There was only one God Kialessa knew with that symbol: The Eternal. Suddenly curious, Kialessa stopped struggling. For just an instant she thought she saw a little white sparkle dance around the edges of some of those leaves. For just a breath, Kia remembered the calm she felt at the shrine.

Allastassia smiled in wicked victory, and began to craft a skilled enchantment spell:

'Burning, lighting, fire and might,
Showing, turning, setting right.
Scarring, wounding, revealing pyre,
Uncover sin with holy fire!'

She shouted, and the ring burst into white fire that curled around her fingers.

                 By Dr Joseph Ireland "Dr Joe"

'Now demon, let everyone see what you really are,' she said. She thrust the circle painfully against Kialessa's forehead.

'No! Ow, ow, ow!' Kialessa said as the circle pressed against her. But it did not burn.

Allastassia looked puzzled.

Kialessa looked puzzled. 'No burning,' she stated, a little surprised.

'Uncover sin with holy fire!' Allastassia shouted again, pouring all her enchantress powers into the circle. It burst into a bright white flame again, even brighter than before, and she pushed it down hard onto Kialessa's forehead.

'Ouch, ouch, ouch!' Kialessa shouted loudly, refusing to cry.

It hurt, but the magic fire did not burn, even though the white flames licked all around her head, her pillow, and her little horns. 'Stop it!' Kialessa shouted, and Allastassia snatched her hands away.

'I don't understand,' one of the girls said.

'Why didn't it burn?' another asked. 'You said it would burn.'

There was a pause while they waited for the auburn girl's answer, but none came.

'Does this mean she's not evil?' the first girl pondered out loud.

That made Allastassia angrier than ever, and without any warning she threw the heavy platinum circle at Kialessa's head. It whacked into her forehead causing terrible pain, and she began to bleed almost right away.

Kialessa burst into tears, and tore her hands and feet away from the quiet girls. She almost threw Allastassia off, and then ran out of the room cradling her head and crying.

She didn't hear what they said as she ran out.

It did not take too long to find the headmistress, but it took a long time for the old woman to finally get the story out of Kialessa. Eventually two of the other girls from the dormitory came out and told the whole story: that Allastassia and some other girls had held Kialessa down and tried to burn her, and then hit her on the head with a religious symbol.

They put Kialessa to bed in the kitchen that night. She curled up against the stove, her feet among the dancing fire of the coals, a thick woolly carpet for a blanket on a bed of soft, welcome straw.

***

The next morning there was hell to pay. Whatever pathetic lie Allastassia and her gang had tried to build up was quietly quashed by the other thirty silent and frightened witnesses to her brutality. Her parents, nobles of the state, were called in under great humiliation.

The headmistress was livid. She took great personal insult that a student had been physically assaulted in her care. The trial and accusations went on for most of the morning. Parents and tutors shouted behind closed doors, while the two girls sat, unspeaking, in the hall. The steward, ever willing to please the king, seemed to take great concern to involve himself in Kialessa's defence.

Neither girl saw the inside of the college the whole day.

In the end, the other four girls all got kitchen duty for a week and, as the children of nobles, they were all humiliated. How it

     By Dr Joseph Ireland "Dr Joe"

made Kialessa laugh! Allastassia and her parents were made to apologise publicly to Kialessa and to the college, and her father had to pay the high priestess to heal the little scar on her forehead.

But Kialessa refused healing. It was more than her head that was injured. She no longer felt safe to sleep in the girls' dormitory. For the rest of the afternoon, she first simmered in anger, then shouted in rage at the adults for their failure. To her dark satisfaction it complicated things for them. There were classes that had to be rearranged to keep the girls separate, and suitable sleeping requirements sorted out. None of them seemed to think the kitchen was appropriate, but clearly they didn't know how long ovens kept their warmth.

She was used to dealing with other people's fear regarding her nature and appearance, but she'd always felt safe in the dormitory at night. She had done nothing to this girl, not even tried to steal her so-called 'boyfriend'. But she'd been held down and hit on the head during the night by her and her friends.

She wanted everyone to know that. She wanted them to know what kind of person the pretty perfect princess really was: a pretty, perfect *bully*.

She wanted everyone to hate Allastassia just as much as she did. She got her first chance that evening; after the adults had stopped shouting at each other, and after the humiliated father had struck his daughter's hands with a reed right in front of them all. It was after the head mistress had sighed softly and declared they all put this uncomfortable business behind them and that they all go prepare for dinner. That was when Kialessa snuck out after the auburn girl and her mother, as they headed out into the garden.

She wanted to know what the girl really thought. She wanted

to hear something that she could use against her one day. The mother and her daughter sat on a stone bench in one of the gardens, their backs against a thick hedge that would hide Kialessa well. Pressing past some guards she crept into the gardens till she could hear them talk.

For a long time, they were silent.

'My hands hurt,' the pretty princess moaned.

Kialessa almost burst out laughing. She had to cover her mouth to stop from making a noise. The mother turned, but Kialessa was certain she didn't see her in her hiding place.

'I know,' her mother commiserated. 'They probably will for a time.'

Then after another pause the mother continued in a gentle voice, 'Allastassia, why did you do that?'

Allastassia started crying soft tears again. She looked up at her mother. 'She's a demon, Mother. Why didn't the fire burn her?'

Her mother sighed. 'That enchantment I taught you is quite powerful, Allastassia. It pierces many defences to reveal evil creatures. Unless that girl is a demon more powerful than all the forces in the king's hall, she's simply not evil.'

Allastassia cried some more. Clearly, she couldn't believe that Kialessa was a powerful demon, and that meant she'd made a terrible mistake, a mistake she might even regret.

'I'm so sorry, Mother. I thought all Tae'anaryl were evil.'

'I've taught you better than to judge a person by their appearance, my dear. That is one of the most important skills for a noble, or an enchantress. We expected more from you,' she chastened her daughter in a gentle voice.

     By Dr Joseph Ireland "Dr Joe"

They were piercing words, Kialessa knew. A parent's disappointment could sting much more than a father's angry hand.

It made the girl cry some more, but Kialessa wasn't enjoying it as much now. She hadn't realised that Allastassia might have actually been acting out of fear, not hatred. It was just like Piex had said about the rude boy. Allastassia was afraid of Kialessa. Perhaps she was more a frightened girl than a bully.

Suddenly Allastassia asked, 'Mother, did a demon really kill Uncle Tomi?'

'Yes dear.'

'When I grow up, I'm going to kill every demon in the land.'

The mother sat her up and held her daughter's hands. 'Allastassia, you listen to me. Revenge is a terrible thing. It cannot be satisfied. I have travelled from one end of this land to the other and crossed swords with brigands and tyrants. I've matched spells with dragons and wild fey. And I've seen men, dwarves and angels fall because of their desire for revenge. Don't ever let revenge be your motivation. Justice yes, but revenge, no. It will destroy you. If you cannot show mercy to your enemies you are already lost to the path of what is good. And you never know when your mercy may rekindle the love of goodness in the heart of a lost soul. I've lived to see it, many times.'

She paused to look in her daughter's eyes, and then continued her little speech. 'Revenge breeds revenge, and kindness acts of mercy. Goodness creates goodness, and hatred follows hatred. Give what you want more of. Haven't we taught you that?'

'Mother, what does it mean to be good?' the young

enchantress asked.

Her mother thought for a moment before answering. 'In our world, goodness can be bottled and shaped into forms of beauty and light. Goodness exists everywhere that evil does not, and evil flees from it, if it can perceive it at all. But goodness is … goodness means … hmm. That's one of the hard questions. I believe the archpriest, Theglios of the god Serros, taught that the true essence of goodness is simply this: to do to other people what you would have them do to you, if you were in their place,' she said.

Despite herself, tears welled up in Kialessa's eyes. With all her heart, she wished she had a mother that could teach her such things. The only thing her mother had taught her was how to steal coins from other people's pockets when they weren't looking. And people never seemed to like that.

'I guess I would not want to be held down and attacked, unless I actually *did* something wrong,' Allastassia admitted at last. 'I am sorry we did that to Kialessa.'

'Then I hope you will tell her,' her mother replied.

But Kialessa wasn't going to wait to let Allastassia be the first to make peace. She was going to treat Allastassia the way she wished Allastassia had treated her in the first place. She edged out of the garden as the mother and daughter continued their conversation, and raced around to the front so that they didn't know she'd been spying on them.

She had intended to hurt Allastassia, to waste her own life trying to make Allastassia unhappy. Now, she realised that was not the person she wanted to become. She was a better person than that, and had better things to do with her time.

She came around to the front of the garden, walking in

boldly, tail swishing from underneath her dress. As she approached the mother roused her daughter, who sat up as quickly as she could and tried to dry her tears before Kialessa noticed.

'Allastassia,' Kialessa announced as soon as she approached, 'how would you like to be friends?'

The enchantress's mouth fell open in speechless surprise. So did her mother's.

'But,' Allastassia said, 'I hit you on the head.'

'I know,' Kialessa said, fingering her little healing scar, 'and … it hurt. But don't worry about it. I'd rather be friends. I think we'd make better friends than enemies.'

Allastassia smiled, and looked up at her mother who nodded her approval. Leaping from her chair Allastassia hugged her.

'I'm sorry I hit you on the head, Kialessa. It was wrong. It must have really hurt.'

'It did, and being held down is terrifying … but I forgive you.' Allastassia really did look sorry, and offered her another hug.

'I promise I won't do anything like that ever again!' she said, sounding happy to be free of her guilt.

'Thank you!' Kialessa grinned. 'Thank you very much!'

Kialessa enjoyed spending time with Allastassia for the rest of the afternoon. As for the adults they seemed put out when they learnt they had made peace and there wouldn't have to be changes to the sleeping arrangements and classroom timetables at all. Her father and the headmistress couldn't speak sensibly for a week but, Kialessa reasoned, that is the way it is with adults at times.

As for the girls, Kialessa tried to teach her to balance on a stone, which Allastassia was terrible at. For her part Allastassia had a little glass wand which she used to craft amazingly realistic butterfly illusions, which Kialessa chased around the garden with delight. They found they had a lot in common, despite widely differing upbringings. It wasn't long before Kialessa could see some of the auburn enchantress's good points, for she was good at heart.

And that, though it was always hard for Kialessa to believe, was how she found her third friend.

 By Dr Joseph Ireland "Dr Joe"

The Half Troll

It's hard to see, even at a distance, what a person may become. The young, the foolish, the proud. Turn away and in the blink of an eye a dozen years have passed, and your proud, foolish youth of yesterday have become the heroes of today. What does it take? Time. Just time.

– King Dunnkan, castle records 15.2.312 CY

The next day Kialessa met Posk.

The headmistress interrupted the class to introduce a strange looking young boy. He had green skin, and such long arms he rested his knuckles on the floor. His chest was shaped like a barrel and he was heavily muscled. A single random tusk jutted from his lower jaw. Yet he seemed shy and a little lost, much like Kialessa thought she must have looked on her first day.

'Sometimes,' the headmistress said, 'a younger student will show so much promise, or cause so much trouble, they will be sent up here from the orphanage in town to help them find their place in the world. Posk here, it seems, is a little of both.'

'Posk!' he muttered, as if he was trying to help, but in a voice which clearly indicated education would not be his strong point. The students giggled.

The headmistress glared at them. 'He might show little promise in academic skills, but they assure me his physical skills are far beyond his age. And, to put a stop to rumours before they begin; yes, he was found eight years ago as a toddler at the orphanage in town that raised him. His real name isn't 'Posk', but that is all anybody knows him as, and that was what he calls himself.'

'Posk!' he repeated, grinning as though he'd done something right.

They couldn't help but laugh. Half trolls were famous for their … well, stupidity. Normally half trolls were lucky if they made the lower ranks of the king's army, but it seemed the priests at the orphanage were determined to civilise this wild boy, and had sponsored him so that he could go to the college. Posk, for his part, seemed far more interested in watching a dust bunny scurry along the floor. Kialessa imagined he'd love nothing more than to leap on it.

Yet as he joined in the activities of the day, it soon became apparent that Posk was not only distracted, but he was also severely mentally handicapped. He had a vocabulary of about six words which he used with different emphasis to mark different occasions. He didn't know which way to hold a book, and there was no point teaching him how to read. If the tutor didn't stop him, he was quite happy to take a drink out of a dirty sink, and couldn't see what all the fuss was about when he did.

But as is the way with half trolls at times, he was also gifted

     By Dr Joseph Ireland "Dr Joe"

with immense strength.

Inhuman strength.

Posk broke something hourly. The other students complained, and told him off to his face, but Kialessa didn't. She didn't think he broke things because he was careless, he just didn't understand his own strength. Posk was having a terrible time fitting in, just like she had at first. She felt so sorry for him, and tried to look out for him so that he didn't get into trouble.

Nothing serious happened, at least not until the third day. Posk was fine for about an hour. He listened, watched and tried to copy the strange symbols from the board. Then he snapped. Or rather, his stylus snapped: the little wooden pencil they all used to scratch words into the slate plates.

With a tremendous roar he smashed the slate on the desk. Students screamed and ran in all directions. The tutor started shouting, and that only seemed to make Posk angrier and more confused. He started throwing desks around.

Darrix got involved then, and with a calm and deliberate gesture he grabbed up a chair and prevented a desk or two from flying into the wall. He spoke in a firm yet quiet voice to Posk, who shouted and roared in confused, guttural speech. Something he said must have gotten through because, instead of throwing desks, Posk banged his fists on the ground.

'I think he's going to attack you,' Piex said, cringing behind a chair.

Kialessa had leapt up onto a broken desk, trying also to calm the savage boy. 'Just keep talking to him, Darrix!' she shouted.

'I'm trying!' Darrix shouted back, and Posk roared.

'Look out!' Allastassia shouted from where she was pinned

down by upturned desks. Everyone else had fled from the room, except the tutor who sat, dazed, in the corner.

Posk bent into a dangerous-looking crouch, as if he was about to jump and attack someone. Piex cast some kind of spell at Posk with nervous, shaking hands and it fizzled out without effect. Allastassia tried using some of her enchantress powers, willing him to sleep. But the enraged boy shrugged it off and leapt at her with an angry snarl.

He will break her arm without even realising it, Kia thought. Darrix was too far away to stop him, but raced to try to tackle him from behind. At least he stood a ghost of a chance, but Kia wasn't willing to risk harm to come to any of the others. So she brought out her secret. She'd smuggled her father's whip out several days ago, just for company, and to see what she could get away with. She'd been practicing with it quite a bit since weapons training a few weeks ago. With a sudden crack she untwisted it and wrapped it around Posk's thick neck. Using both hands and all her strength she pulled him to the ground in mid-flight.

The force flung her through the air, and she landed half on his chest and half on a fallen chair. Without thinking she gave him an intimidating hiss, her eyes glowing in anger.

Posk stopped fighting and covered his face. He lay on the ground, whimpering.

She'd stopped him.

'Arrum gn gn um,' he mumbled.

'What is it, Posk?' she demanded. They'd been taught that trolls respected strength, and did not respond well to gentle requests.

He held up his hand to her. There, jammed up under a

fingernail, with what must have been excruciating pain, was the sharp end of the stylus.

The four friends let out a sympathetic sigh.

'Poor Posk!' Allastassia muttered.

'Let me help you,' Kia said. As gently as possible she began to pull the splinter from his finger.

'Hold still!' she ordered.

Posk shouted out as the splinter was removed, but then fell silent as Darrix held his hand and muttered a prayer to his god. The finger still bled, but Posk was as calm as dawn.

'I think my God removed the pain,' Darrix said, wondering out loud.

Posk stumbled to his feet. He wrapped his arms around Darrix, then Kia, and then he patted Allastassia. With a sad look he surveyed the terrible damage he'd wrought on the room in under a moment.

'It's all right,' Kialessa told him. 'We'll help cl–'

Just then two armoured castle guards burst into the room, weapons drawn. They looked angry, and were terrifying.

Posk flung himself to the floor trembling and babbling. He begged, although he had no words to use. Kialessa realised the whip was still around his neck as, with pleading sobs, he tugged at it and waited on all fours.

'I think we need to take him,' a guard said.

Posk bellowed and shook his head. He tugged the whip again but did not remove it.

'What's he trying to say?' the tutor, still crouching in a corner, asked.

They all looked at the moaning and whimpering boy. He

rested up against Kialessa's leg, and put her foot on his back as though he was a real Posk. He gestured on all fours.

'He wants you to be his master, Kia,' Darrix said, smiling.

'He what?' she said, lip curled in disbelief.

Darrix smiled. 'You brought him low,' he explained. 'He trusts you to help him control himself, and the situation he is in.'

'You mean he wants to be her pet?' Allastassia asked in an indignant voice.

'No, but he wants her to be his keeper.' Darrix smiled.

'Oh, I know what this is!' Piex suddenly stuttered. '*Tauira-Toa*! Warrior's apprentice! Half-troll children often take a master to subdue them till they are of age. It gives them some freedom to make mistakes while they are learning. It's an important cultural difference between them and the elves –'

'Right,' Allastassia interrupted. 'He wants to be her slave then.'

'No, no, not slave. More like student or helper … or, servant, I suppose.'

Kialessa smiled at the young, worried boy.

'Sure, I'll be his master,' she said. 'I know what it's like to be alone in a new college.'

Allastassia looked dubious. The guards looked confused. The tutor looked frightened.

'We'll need to take–' the guard began.

'No, you will not!' Kialessa argued, with hands on hips.

Darrix interjected, his hands help up in a peace-making gesture. 'The half-troll student is new, and needs proper training in our ways. Kialessa has offered to help him on this journey. Please, forgive the interruption to our class? We will be all right

　　　By Dr Joseph Ireland "Dr Joe"

now.' He spoke in a diplomatic voice that was so grown up the guards might have thought him a tutor.

They looked around for the adult and found her, still crouching in the corner.

'Yes, all very nice,' the tutor mumbled in disbelief. 'The tae'anaryn part demon is going to look after the raging half troll and make sure he does the right things.'

She sounded confused and worried. But, for whatever reason, the guards took her at her word and, shrugging their shoulders, walked out. The tutor was too panicked to say anything coherent, and reached out forlornly as they left.

So Posk stayed.

He didn't let Kialessa take the whip off all afternoon. He didn't let her take it off all day. And that evening, after dinner, the college students were treated to the singularly unusual sight of a tae'anaryn girl riding a half troll boy, standing barefoot up on his hips as he ran on knuckles and feet; a whip around his musclebound neck her only bridle. The adults were scandalised, the children entertained, and the tae'anaryn girl ecstatic as she giggled in wild delight while he leapt and ran and frolicked.

And that was how she found her fourth friend.

***

7 Friends can come in all shapes and sizes, but they can still make a real difference in your world

That evening, creeping alone among the rafters for conversations to listen to, Kialessa heard something very interesting. The captain and the high priestess were discussing things when along came the steward.

'I'm surprised to see you two up and about. I would have thought King Dunnkan would have too many duties for you to keep you from chatting in the alleys!' he teased with a smile in his voice. Kialessa noticed he was holding the rod of the king deep within his robes – perhaps he always carried it with him?

'You can talk,' the captain replied in his loud voice.

'Remember the mines of Draconspit? Kept you up all night for weeks!'

'Must you bring that up every time?' the priestess complained.

'It's all right, High Priestess,' the steward muttered, just a little sarcastically. He seemed to be in a far more playful than his usual self. 'The good captain here just misses the former days, when his sword was *actually* used.'

'Ha! And I know your skills are still put to daily use,' he retorted, but smiled. It seemed they'd known each other before they came to work for King Dunnkan.

'Still,' the captain mused, 'those were good days. No walls to tend. No whingey castle guards to watch over. Good days.'

'Indeed, they were,' the priestess replied.

'If only that little bookish wizard–' the steward began.

'I see my timing, once more, is impeccable.' The wizard's quiet voice came from the shadows.

'Ha!' the captain boomed. 'We were just about to speak of you, Wizard! Whatever are you doing hiding there?'

'Ah, Captain,' the priestess muttered, 'you know better than to question a wizard's motives.'

'Like when we found him knee deep in a bog trying to find some swamp weed. I do remember that!' the captain boomed in good natured humour, and they all laughed.

But the steward looked concerned. 'Perhaps a questioning of motives isn't out of hand, given the current circumstances.'

'Whatever do you mean?' the wizard said. Kialessa thought he sounded concerned.

'Not that I would accuse any of you,' the steward explained, 'but I would remind you that the intruder bypassed the magical barriers on both outer and inner walls. One way he could have done that was to be … invited.'

'What exactly are you trying to say?' the captain said. He looked dangerous.

'Nothing. Simply asking. I don't mean to accuse.'

'But you do, yet again, don't you?' the priestess said. 'Again, your distrust drives you test us, failing to trust even yourself. Must you to clutch at shadows once more?'

Kialessa thought the mood became a bit tense.

The wizard sighed. 'This is just like the ruins of *Civita Aurea* all over again,' he muttered.

The captain laughed and then they were silent once more.

'I am assured of our honesty. Even yours, Steward,' the priestess said in the silence.

He sighed. 'Yes, yes, I … must apologise,' the steward muttered. 'It has been a tense time since the intruder was first spotted by that little tae'anaryn girl. Twice now, yet we still have no leads.'

'Ah yes, the tae'anaryn,' the priestess mused.

'Well, well, speak your thoughts!' the captain insisted. 'Don't leave us hanging now.'

She sighed. It seemed to Kialessa as if the priestess enjoyed the spotlight just a little. 'I find her of a kind heart, much more than I would have expected from one of her –'

'Race?' the steward interrupted in an unkind tone.

'No,' she replied flatly, 'upbringing. She is generous, quick to observe, and she keeps her word.'

'I agree,' the wizard replied, 'I have had little cause to

mistrust her, and she seems ever willing to help her friends.'

'Bah! Even the most black-hearted scoundrel is willing to help their friends!' the steward almost hissed.

'True, but I believe her heart to be good,' the priestess said.

'That's a relief! We've enough to worry about, what with the supplies for soldiers on rounds.' The captain shook his head. 'But, tell us, does she bear the sign?'

'Indeed, this is important,' the wizard chimed in.

Again, the priestess paused, perhaps just trying to place her words, scratching her neat little beard. 'She has passed every test I have placed her in, and many more.'

That made Kialessa wonder: what tests?

'But does she bear the sign?' the steward insisted.

'The divinations are clear for her, much clearer than I have experienced in many years. Yes. She bears the sign in her soul.'

There was a mutter of disbelief, and everyone looked over at the steward. As for her part Kialessa had no idea what they were talking about.

'Just like you, eh Steward?' the captain said in a sober voice.

The steward sighed. 'Well, it's not like she's the first. Every decade or so another crops up. But I've never failed my position. The gods have taken care of that. Besides, are we not all united in this cause?'

'True, true!' the captain agreed, but the wizard and priestess were silent.

'What becomes of her?' the wizard asked the priestess.

'We'll just have to wait and see,' she said, 'and watch her choices for now. I cannot see beyond her immediate destiny, but I do know she is destined to influence the lives of many, as she already has simply by being here. We will have to await King Dunnkan's decision.'

'I wish King Dunnkan had given her another year with her parents,' the steward complained. 'He had promised but, after the dog attack, he felt she'd be safer here. Now you have confirmation that she bears the sign? Well, that is good. Perhaps the two of us together might finally be able to keep King Dunnkan out of trouble … most of the time.'

He smiled, as if it was supposed to be a joke. But the others looked serious as though protecting the king was worth more to them than their own lives. It was what everyone was supposed to think in their land, but they looked as if they really took it to heart. Then Kialessa remembered something. They'd never formally, with binding magic, made her take the oath to protect the king, and she hoped it wouldn't matter one day. And what was this sign about? Was it some kind of birthmark? Or was the steward a tae'anaryn as well?

'Steward,' the priestess said, interrupting Kialessa's thoughts, 'she merely has the sign, not the office. She is so very young. I doubt the gods would ask it of her, not for many years, if at all.'

Kialessa's mind was racing. Why had no one told her about this before? Were they all keeping secrets, and why? Was it to protect her, or did they fear what she might become? And how was she and that bossy steward connected by some sign? She adjusted her position among the rafters, promising herself she'd get some answers soon.

'Ah, remember when it was just us four?' The steward changed the conversation topic. 'Not all this fancy intrigue. All this … formal name calling.'

     By Dr Joseph Ireland "Dr Joe"

'That's for your own protection Grud … I mean, Steward,' the priestess smiled. So, she did have a sense of humour.

'Cutting through the wilderness, braving ancient mines. Those were days of adventure!' the captain continued.

'Indeed, they were,' the wizard smiled at the memory.

The captain laughed. 'Did you hear how she's made a friend of that new half-troll boy? Quite the little team they've got going in their training classes, eh? Seems the mantle of Lenmer'el's next heroes may yet pass to those our priestess deems too young.'

She scoffed, but the steward smiled and told her, 'Yes, you of all people know the gods can be expected to work in unexpected ways. She may surprise you. We may all surprise you before this trouble with the intruder is well and truly over.'

'Let us hope that is true,' the wizard smiled as though joking that the steward was somehow not measuring up to his expectations.

But the steward smiled back, patting him on the shoulder. 'We have tarried too long here,' he said with a sad tone, 'and we've a great man's kingdom to run.'

They agreed and said their goodbyes. It had seemed such a friendly meeting, and Kialessa was amazed at how much she'd learnt. After a moment the steward was left standing alone.

Then Kialessa caught her breath as he turned and looked right up at her. He must have somehow known she was there, but for how long, she could not tell. Perhaps the whole conversation was just for her.

When he spoke, it was quiet and sincere, as though he was talking to an adult. 'I trust, Kialessa, you know how to keep a secret?' He did not smile as he spoke, and then walked briskly away.

 By Dr Joseph Ireland "Dr Joe"

Some say the greatest evil is to kill for sport, others say the greatest evil is to speak ill of the king. I say the greatest evil is to do nothing when a wrong ought to be righted!

– Humdug: dwarf scholar

Kialessa tried to tell Piex about the strange conversation she'd heard, but he didn't understand castle intrigue. He fixated on the fact that she'd gone around spying on people, again, and hadn't gotten into trouble for it. He didn't have anything to add about the sign the priestess was talking about, and had no idea how she and the steward might have it. He promised to investigate it, when he got the time, which Kialessa thought would be never.

She didn't want to tell Darrix yet; he wouldn't be impressed. And Allastassia, well, Kialessa just didn't know how well she could keep a secret.

She didn't tell anyone that they'd known about her, and

Kialessa was puzzled enough to find out more. However, she knew she couldn't ask directly. She didn't want the others to know she was unintentionally spying on them. She remembered how King Dunnkan had told her that he'd been watching her all her life, yet how? He'd known about the dog attack, she promised to ask him how the next time they got the chance to chat.

What had really worried both Kialessa and Piex, however, was the steward's suggestion that the intruder must have had some inside help. Who on earth would willingly betray the king like that? Or, if not willingly, then who would have had the power to force someone to do it? It was no wonder the steward was clutching at shadows.

With no answers and nothing but questions Kialessa went back to work for a while, yet she felt in her heart that the answers would soon present themselves. The captain was right about one thing: they were five good friends.

At the headmistress' order Posk spent most mornings out running in the forest and only came in for lunch. Afterwards he would watch the goings on at the college with great curiosity, joining in as often as he could. He would usually bridle himself as soon as he entered, making sure that the tutors could see he was safe and obedient. Kialessa thought he was pure at heart and didn't want to accidentally hurt anyone, or make any enemies. Posk could hit things very hard. He just needed someone to point him in the right direction.

And he was so strong! He seemed happy to walk around with her sitting on his back like some kind of portable chair for hours. Within a few days his presence was tolerated at the college, and many people seemed to even forget he was there. And, with her new friends and a bridled half-troll in tow, no one seemed to want to tease her anymore.

Piex was as studious as ever and Kialessa had to interrupt him if she wanted his help, or to know something. Most of the other students were happy to help her learn how to read now, so she felt she was progressing well. It was sad though, that most of them ignored Piex so they had no idea what an enormous amount of knowledge he held about everything! She was determined to help him find as many spells as possible so they could have more adventures together. Maybe one day he would learn how to turn her invisible. Then she could really sneak around and find out who was helping the intruder!

As for Allastassia, after she discovered she could not be Kialessa's enemy, she seemed to devote herself to giving Kialessa a social make-over. She had all her friends arranging Kialessa's hair and dress, and Kialessa even tolerated it in the name of being social. They put little gem clips on her hair and tied it back with expensive silk ribbons. Allastassia's gang even tried to figure out a way to help her hide her horns; till she insisted that they were a part of her and not to be hidden in any way.

The popular girls were all very quiet for a moment, till one of them spoke up. 'Well, she's definitely a summer complexion. That means you need to wear bright colours...' she said, changing the subject. None of them ever brought up the idea of how to hide horns again.

Kialessa learnt a lot from them about dress, social standards and how to speak like a noble. Deep down she knew that it was because of the enchantress's approval that she finally began to fit in with all the girls, though many of them liked her already but were too shy to show it. It was ironic, but it was Allastassia's mistake that had helped convince the few remaining sceptics

Kialessa wasn't evil; that it was all right to talk to her, and maybe even be her friend. She was grateful for that.

Darrix, for his part, was just as busy being social, leading many of the training battles and helping the other young warriors every day. Not many of them knew of his intense devotion to The Eternal, though he did not keep it secret. He was at the shrine every morning, and almost all day on Serrosdays. Kialessa would join him then, and participate in the discussions and singing. It was nice, and she enjoyed their company; Darrix's in particular. The others at the shrine made her feel welcome. The priestess in charge was gentle, with wise words, deep thoughts, and a positive outlook. It was a welcome break from study, and Kialessa found the devotions refreshed her.

One day, Darrix surprised her with a little circle made of three leather strips, tied on with a leather strip for a necklace: a tiny symbol of the circle of The Eternal.

'It's for you,' he said.

Her mouth was wide in wonder. Was he giving her a gift? Was someone giving her a gift they'd made *just for her*?

'For … if you need to pray,' he muttered, turning just a little red with embarrassment.

She laughed and held his arm. 'Thank you,' she said, and put the necklace on right away.

Some of the adults at the shrine teased him about the gift, but she kept it close to her heart. It was as much to remember her friendship with Darrix as to bring herself closer to the first god whom she'd ever felt had shown a genuine interest in her.

College was going well, even if she only had one dress to wear. But as a daughter of an inn-keep, not a noble, it was

By Dr Joseph Ireland "Dr Joe"

tolerated. Still, her venture into shorts during studies of athletics and physical prowess had brought permanent change. The headmistress had berated the Gedzelai tutor, who'd been red-faced and adamant that Kialessa was to attend in shorts. Eventually, they hit on a compromise and, with a pair of scissors, needle and thread, the headmistress herself had sewn a swathe of fabric around those shorts so that they looked like skirts.

'Skorts!' Kialessa had pronounced as soon as the old headmistress held them up for her to see, and all the other girls in the dormitory giggled.

'No, they're Studies of Athletics and Physical Prowess shorts for girls,' the headmistress insisted.

But the name stuck, and skorts became very popular. Within a week they were being made all over town for the college students and other children. Some even were sold for three silver pieces each to the eager nobles, whose life seemed to revolve around dressing their children in all the latest fashions.

In time Kialessa even began to forget that there had been an intruder about. *Let the steward worry about it,* she reasoned. Life was good and the college was tough, and the five of them worked hard together. Their favourite class, at least together, was Studies of Athletics and Physical Prowess. The tutor was fond of preparing obstacle courses, and they often played games as he found new ways to challenge them.

'I'm with Piex,' Kialessa would say.

'I'm with Kia,' Darrix would say.

'I'm with Darrix,' Allastassia would say.

Posk didn't say anything. He went where Kialessa went.

So the five of them formed a team to face whatever challenge the tutor had devised. Sometimes they would face off against other teams to capture flags, or they would have to help each other across strange obstacles to claim victory, or they would face off against the tutor to achieve their goals.

Within three weeks they had won every prize. It got to the point that no other student teams were willing to take them on, even if it was everyone else versus their team. They tried splitting them up among the other teams, but no one was really happy with that solution. Besides, battle training at the college was *supposed* to be hard. Having a powerful enchantress, talented wizard, prayerful warrior, a raging half troll, and Kialessa was too much for them all.

'What will we call ourselves?' Darrix asked.

'Allastassia's Army,' the enchantress immediately suggested.

'I thought Conglomerate of the Allied Races,' Piex said. He'd obviously given this some previous thought.

'Conglomerate … Allied … Races … that's 'car' for short,' Darrix replied. 'Car … Now who ever heard of car?' He laughed in good humour.

It sounded like a strange and silly word; something a bird might say. So they didn't have a name yet, but they were proud of their accomplishments. That was, until the tutor had decided they needed a serious challenge and made them compete with the senior students.

'Senior students!' they'd chorused in disbelief.

The Gedzelai tutor had nodded in sober reply.

It did not go well. They were defeated in seconds. Posk was intimidated, and an archer with darts was so quick and accurate Piex and Allastassia didn't even get a spell off. Kialessa was downed trying to cross a rope at the same time as a senior student, even with the help of her tail. Finally, Darrix was knocked unconscious by a burly wrestler. The other group didn't even go on to win.

But the tutor smiled. 'You disappoint me, young ones. You will try again, and you will not stop trying until you win every session!'

Kialessa and her friends didn't win much in the coming weeks, but eventually they did win. Soon, they were afforded a measure of begrudging respect even among the senior students.

'At least the senior students are a challenge,' Piex said, not arrogant, just stating the facts as he saw them.

Kialessa had to agree.

***

Two weeks later it was Planasday once more, and Kialessa was tired. She'd been at the college for over seven weeks now, and usually spent Planasday afternoons exploring the castle, surprising the lazy guards, or simply sitting and learning to read.

Yet this had been a very long Planasday afternoon. She'd followed Darrix and Piex around as they'd hurried along on their chores and curiosities, popping into stores along the main street of the little city that lay outside the castle walls. At first it was interesting, but now she was starting to feel tired.

They found Posk a moment later, scuttling through some old barrels for disused apples, and he was only too happy to tag along. She envied his unbridled sense of irresponsibility. She knew that once he'd had enough, he'd leave. She was ready to leave, too, but she wanted Piex to check over her first twelve-word letter to the king, and Darrix was simply good company, so she'd stayed. For now.

'Come on then,' Darrix said her with an enthusiastic grin. He could tell she'd seen enough and had enough of people in town staring at her. 'One more task to do and then we'll be off.' He marched towards Pringol, the money lender. She'd heard only bad things about him from the other girls at the college. He was a thief who obeyed the king's law so well none could find any fault with him. He was said to charge much for his services, and was merciless to those who could not pay their debts.

'Why are we going in there?' Kialessa asked, a little nervous. Darrix tugged at the little coin purse at his side. Kialessa noticed it hadn't grown any smaller in all the time they'd been about that morning.

'How many coins are in there?' she wondered out loud.

'Couple of hundred,' he whispered with a smile.

'A couple!' She was astounded. How did a young man get away with carrying so much money? And why was the pouch so small?

He smiled, and seemed to know what she was thinking. 'It's an enchanted pouch that keeps its size. Inside there's the recent tithes from the shrine, guarded by sacred prayers. I'm taking the offerings to the moneylender for safe keeping. It's at the priestess' request, and she trusts me to do it because she knows I will.'

Kialessa was still astounded. 'So why didn't we go there straight away?'

'Too many thieves expect to find gold on a priestess, and not a handful of youth that wander all around town first. They'll

     By Dr Joseph Ireland "Dr Joe"

think I'm going to do something for my parents. Look, I even have a note!' He showed her.

The ruse seemed a lot of work to protect some shrine funds, but Kialessa knew that there might be a good reason. In a world full of magic it was difficult to hide personal possessions without magical help, and magical help was always expensive. Most nobles and other rich folk would store their choice belongings with rich friends or money lenders, who no doubt charged them for the service.

Still, it seemed to be an enormous amount of trust the priestess was showing Darrix.

'What are you two talking about?' Piex inquired from up ahead.

'Nothing,' they chorused.

Piex looked a bit put out.

But Kialessa was surprised. Why was she the only one Darrix trusted to tell about the money purse? Piex was a wizard.

A moment later they arrived at Pringol's office. The building where the moneylender worked was built of fine stone, and broad sigils of protection and prosperity inlaid in gold were set into every corner and windowsill. While not the most ornate building in town it looked rich to Kialessa, and solid. An equally well-built and broad dwarven mercenary glared down at them as they entered the front door. He did not let Posk enter.

'Wait here,' she told him.

'Rmmm,' Posk nodded. He seemed to know it would not be a good idea to force the issue.

'No talking inside,' Darrix whispered.

She found the inside practical but opulent. The benches were carved of solid oak, not the weak and fast-growing pine furniture that Allastassia would have complained about. The curtains were thick and luxurious, and the room was scented with a relaxing peach aroma. Soft music played from an enchanted viol, and Kialessa noticed the air was warmer as it wafted from the rear area where Pringol himself worked.

The moneylender was not to be seen, but four pretty and organised female office staff tended to customers.

'Darrix!' A happy voice whispered. It was Allastassia.

'Oh, hello!' he whispered in his friendly manner. 'What brings you here?'

'Mother sent me to keep her sister company while she secured another loan,' she said with an imperious wave of her hand. 'Boring stuff, but she insists I come to learn the ways of other nobles.'

They all sighed at their various thoughts of what the adults thought they needed to learn.

'Anyway, what are – ' she said.

A busy office staff shushed them.

'Sorry!' Allastassia whispered, and continued in such a whisper Kialessa almost couldn't hear her. 'What brings you three in here?'

'I'm with Kia,' Piex said.

'I'm with Darrix,' Kia said.

'Not this again!' Allastassia smiled.

'And I'm going to make a small deposit,' Darrix whispered.

'Really, who for?' she asked him.

'I have this note from my parents,' he said, not really lying, but not answering the question either.

Kialessa hid her surprise. Why would he tell only her what was in the bag?

Without warning their peace and quiet was broken as violent shouts erupted from outside. A thunderous crash echoed and a huge web of golden chains appeared from nowhere to wrap around the dwarven mercenary and pin him to the wall. In the next moment the door burst open.

'Hold your places,' a voice demanded, 'or face *death* at my hands!'

In burst two muscular young warriors, a man in wizard robes, and an archer. They were ill-kempt and unshaven, wearing the rugged forest gear of bandits. They set about disabling any defences the moneylender had, including a bench that jumped to life and tried to attack them. The warriors hacked it to bits in an instant with their battle axes.

People screamed as they lay on the floor, and Kialessa huddled with her friends against the wall. Two of the bandits ran to the rear office and bashed down Pringol's door. Pringol was a fat gnome, no taller than any of them, and his hands bore a dozen gaudy rings as ostentatious as his overdone clothes. He shouted at the bandits who bound him in seconds.

'What do we do?' Kialessa whispered.

'Stay down till they leave and hope they don't hurt anybody,' Darrix instructed.

Two bandits laughed to each other as they shovelled handfuls of coins and treasure into two large sacks.

'What happens to the money?' Kialessa asked.

'Well, Pringol will lose a lot of it, so he'll have to hope no one comes to claim on their investments for a few seasons,' Allastassia replied, looking concerned. 'Otherwise he may have to sell things to meet customers' demands. It could bankrupt him.'

'Doesn't he pay a fee to some larger money lender to help him when things like this happen?' Kialessa asked.

'You mean insurance? No, Pringol is the largest money lender in the city,' she sighed. 'If Pringol goes broke, many, many people stand to lose their investments.'

Thieves. Kialessa scoffed. *They take what isn't theirs and leave others in terrible trouble without caring.* Perhaps the lazy town guard would catch them? No, something had to be done right now, even if they only stalled them long enough for the guards to arrive. The wizard and archer kept their eyes on everyone in the room. The archer had a strange bow, less than half the size of a normal bow, and it sat cross ways along his arm with a thick wooden handle to hold it there. She'd never seen anything like it, but hoped it worked just like any other bow. The wizard stood there, dangerous arcane fire burning in his hands, ready to be thrown at anything, or anyone.

But as Kialessa looked closely she found there was something interesting about this group. They were armed, they were dangerous, they were dressed like bandits, but there was something else, something almost familiar …

They looked young, not really adults, not much more than six or so years older than herself.

'Senior students,' she whispered to herself in triumph. They defeated senior students quite regularly in college. 'Here's the plan,' she said to her friends. 'Allastassia, take out those thugs with your sleeping enchantment. Piex and Darrix, silence that wizard. I'll deal with the archer.'

'But we've no weapons,' Darrix said, eyebrows furrowed with concern.

'This is profoundly unwise,' Piex agreed.

'Hey!' Kia argued. 'We're kids. What're they going to do?'

Allastassia took one look around at the people in the room and nodded, willing to be a hero. 'I'm ready.'

'But what–' Darrix began.

'Go!' Kia whispered. She tore off her father's whip which she had disguised as a belt once more.

With an innocent smile at the wizard Allastassia stood up and began unleashing her magic at the two in Pringol's office.

'Hey!' the archer said, 'stop th–'

He turned his bow around to face the young enchantress, but Kialessa had been waiting. With a sudden crack of her whip, she struck out not at the archer, not at his bow, but at the notched arrow. With profound satisfaction she knocked it to the ground.

'Ludicrous children!' the wizard roared, but he never did get through his first spell. Either it was the way his tongue suddenly swelled up, one of Piex's favourite enchantments, or the way a young fighter suddenly collided with his stomach. Darrix wasn't very old, but he was tall and strong for his age. He knew some kind of wrestling manoeuvre that had the thin and studious wizard pinned in moments. Piex shoved wads of paper in the wizard's mouth to keep him silent.

The archer shouted for the thugs to help out, but there was no reply. He was about to help his wizard, but stopped as he looked around at the room full of hostile citizens. For a moment he just stood there, confused.

Then, with a dark look at them, he turned to run out the door but stopped short when he faced the dark silhouette of a half troll.

It was Posk.

'Move!' the archer ordered.

Posk growled.

Quick as lightning the thief begun to load an arrow, but Kialessa hit it from his hands once more. He looked at her and she hissed back.

Suddenly he drew a dagger and tried to rush through Posk, and in the same moment Posk threw himself at the archer with both fists raised high in the air.

The archer was struck in the chest and flew back several metres against the wooden boards of the moneylender's bench. His head hit it with a thunderous crunch and he was knocked out cold.

Posk shuffled left and right, unsure of what to do next.

'Hold the wizard,' Kialessa said.

He ran over and nearly crushed Piex in a headlock. 'Not that one!' Kialessa shouted.

Posk dropped Piex chest first on the ground and grabbed the thief wizard on the ground in an iron clad grip. He held on so tight the poor thief couldn't breathe and promptly passed out, though the thick wad of papers in his mouth no doubt helped.

The town guard were there in less than a moment and carted the thieves off to jail. As soon as they untied Pringol and removed his gag, he started shouting. He blamed the town; he blamed his mercenaries. He even blamed Posk for putting a sizeable crack in his darling woodwork. He had them all thrown out immediately and without gratitude.

Thankfully, the mayor of the city was much kinder. The next

day, in a private meeting, he gave them all a handshake, a small medallion and three gold coins each. Kialessa was giddy with delight. She was holding almost half a season's wage for an adult!

Piex smiled, and added his to a small fund he kept in order to buy a blank spell book of his very own. Now, he informed her, added to the ninety-six bronze and four silver he already had, there were only forty-six gold coins to go, which would no doubt take him the best part of his early wizarding life.

'It's one reason why there are so few wizards,' Piex said, sounding sorrowful.

Darrix and Allastassia looked at their coins, unimpressed. Darrix gave all his at the poor box of the next shrine they came across, and Allastassia casually mentioned saving up for a new outfit. Nobles, and some merchant families, were very rich compared to everyone else in Lenmer'el.

Posk found his coins were no good for eating and left them on the floor. Kialessa picked them up and decided to look after them for him.

They may have done great things, and were kindly rewarded, but as Darrix pointed out the mayor had offered no ceremony or celebration to announce their accomplishments. Allastassia suggested the mayor didn't want everyone to know that a group of junior college students had bested his well-trained town guard and Pringol's bank security. The mayor could have acknowledged them in public but didn't even do that.

Also, the headmistress, for reasons of her own, did not tell them off. Instead she took the opportunity to release a public statement claiming the need for the king's college and the good it did, although she didn't name them in person. Many citizens smiled and thanked them wherever they went.

It was the first real danger they'd ever faced.

Figure 8 Kialessa at the castle of Lenmer'el – By Emily Ireland

 By Dr Joseph Ireland "Dr Joe"

The Dream Walker

In a dream, we can create any world of our imagining. Is the real world so different?

– High King Malkom. Royal records. 14.4.318 CY

That night Kialessa had an unexpected and strange dream. She dreamed of Kiel, her adopted brother. He was out picking berries, like they often did, but it was evening, although the light was strange and seemed to come from everywhere.

'Oh, hey Kialessa, glad you could finally make it. I haven't seen you here before,' he said. It seemed odd. They'd been there a hundred times. 'How's the king's college?'

His voice was strange, not at all afraid like it usually was. He seemed calm and peaceful. She wondered how he'd found her.

'It's all right,' she replied, wondering what he was picking because she couldn't see any berries. 'It was hard at first, but I've found some good friends.'

'Yes, the half dragon, the boy priest, the dryad and troll. I know.'

'You know? How could you know them?' she wondered.

'I visit you; you know. You're having a dream.'

'A dream?' Kialessa said. 'Why am I dreaming about you?'

He laughed. 'People usually ask me that and most often they forget me in the morning. Sometimes I forget, too. But in here I remember. I remember I've been visiting people in their dreams for my whole life, Kialessa.'

'Really?'

'You say that every time,' he smiled.

'So, why are we here?'

'I brought you here,' he replied. 'I heard you worrying. What happened today?'

'Oh! We caught some bandits!' she said, her chin held high.

He didn't look impressed. 'You should keep out of trouble!' he said, with a familiar whinging tone. It was Kiel all right.

'We'll be fine!' she boasted.

'Still, I'll go check up on them. I'll see if they've forgiven you,' he said. Kialessa wasn't sure what worried her more: that he could be so confident about finding people in their dreams, or that he still insisted on looking out for her from so far away. How long had he been doing this?

'How *are* you doing this?' she said.

'It's something I do. I've been trying to reach you but you seemed so distracted.'

In the end she decided that, if it was all a dream, it didn't matter anyway. It was still nice to talk to Kiel. 'How are things at home?'

He smiled. 'Mum and Dad are all right, your mum and dad

that is. I'm safe and everything is just the way it always is at the inn. Mum hired a new girl … well, woman really. She's always teasing the customers. It's embarrassing.'

Kialessa laughed at the thought of him being embarrassed.

'Besides, there's something else you really need to know. You know that dream you had with those men who threatened the king? Just the day before you left?'

Suddenly, she did remember. 'You know about that?'

'Only in my dreams,' he said in a sad tone. 'But I was in that dream, too. I brought you to that place where they make the plans. I wanted you to hear what they were saying.'

'But, how? I mean, why?'

He smiled. 'Just 'cause.'

'Why didn't you tell me you could do this when I was at home?' she demanded.

'I did! I tried all the time! But you've only just started to listen this year, when your *life* is in danger!' He looked upset.

'All right. I'm sorry. I'm here now. What do you want me to do?'

He looked surprised. 'No one's ever asked me that before.'

Suddenly the sky wrapped up and they found themselves in a dark place. It was so dark she could hardly see her hand in front of her face. But there were people out there; she could sense them.

'Worked really well this time. It's not usually this easy,' he whispered, more to himself than to her.

'I wish –' Kialessa began, but Kiel cut her off.

'Shh! They're here already. They might hear you.'

'Really?' she wondered, but supposed he had more experience with this dream thing than her. She always did think him a little lost in daydreams. Now she knew why.

She heard a name then, someone was speaking, but she wasn't concentrating and didn't catch what it was. They both started listening to the darkness as carefully as they could.

'… failed me twice now,' someone demanded. It was the powerful voice from her first dream. Now she understood that it was Kiel that had brought her here then, and had brought her here again.

'I am sorry, your **highness**,' the smooth voice replied once more, deep with sarcasm. 'You'll never guess, but one of the little children from the college was breaking the rules and spotted us trying to poison the king's salt. But let's face it; it is only a minor setback to our plans.'

'Which child?' the powerful voice demanded.

'Oh, it doesn't matter,' the smooth voice replied.

Shadows and silhouettes were forming in the void. Kialessa thought they were standing in some kind of large rectangular room, surrounded by towering pillars of stone. There were more than two people in there, she could tell. She had no idea where the smooth voice was coming from, but the powerful voice was coming from the figure of a man. He seemed to turn his back on the others, pouring himself a drink.

'It matters very much,' the powerful voice muttered, sounding so close that Kialessa could almost feel his breath, and she stifled a gasp.

'What of the others? The elves?'

An unfamiliar voice replied, 'They are coming over to our way of thinking.'

'Good. Then we must act soon. Don't let this setback stop

     By Dr Joseph Ireland "Dr Joe"

you. Are the other plans in order?' he demanded.

'Of course!' the smooth voice replied.

'Then don't delay any longer. You must take action soon. Pah! Curse the man who gave permission for Lenmer'el to be a separate kingdom! They are too independent, thinking for themselves. Remove this thorn in my side. Act as soon as you are able. The crown prince is young, and easily intimidated. With the death of their king the hearts of the people will falter, and the strength of their kingdom will be easily called away to war in other lands. You know what we must do!'

'The King of Lenmer'el will die before the spring's end,' the smooth voice promised with a growl.

There was a pause, as if the one with the powerful voice was waiting for them to realise something he already knew.

'And this time if the tae'anaryn stands in your way?' he asked.

'She is no threat,' the smooth voice replied.

'*Kill her*,' the powerful voice demanded.

Kialessa gasped, and Kiel held tightly on to her hand. She couldn't believe they were after …

'Wait!' the powerful voice suddenly said.

'What is it, my liege?'

'Someone is here. Someone uninvited …'

Just then the shadow that belonged to the powerful voice reached out to touch her, and she only just pulled away in time. In that moment she thought she saw the hint of green in his eyes, the touch of deep flaming red on his horns.

'Who is it?' the smooth voice asked.

'Children,' the powerful voice explained, and he began to

whisper something that sounded both potent and evil.

'Oh, I hate it when this happens,' Kiel muttered. He began to pull Kialessa away as quickly as he could.

'When what happens?' Kialessa said.

'Dream hounds,' the powerful voice whispered.

Sinister energy began to gather around them, and it seemed as though a million tiny threads began to wrap around Kialessa and Kiel's hands and arms.

Kiel screamed. 'Run Kialessa! We've got to get out now!'

She didn't need to be told a second time. They turned and ran, screaming. She found herself clawing her way up some kind of hill, scrambling across sharp rocks. She and Kiel ran right to a cliff, and she turned around to find half a dozen shadowy dogs chasing after her.

'What do we do now?' she screamed at Kiel. This was more than she'd bargained for. 'How did he know?'

'Some just do,' he said. 'Look, Kialessa, we need to wake up. They can't find us in the waking world.'

The hounds were sniffing about. They seemed unable to see them, and they were only a few paces away from them. 'Wake up, wake up, wake up!' she repeated to herself.

Kiel looked puzzled. 'Not like that,' he said, and pulling an enormous kite out of thin air he launched them from the cliff face.

The last of the spider strands fell from their ankles, but some of the hounds turned into enormous bestial hawks and began to pursue them.

'What's taking you so long? Wake up!' he told her.

'I'm trying!' she screamed.

'You're doing it all wrong!'

The birds called out then, and began to zero in on them. 'Hide here!' he said, and wrapped the kite around them. She found herself hiding in the attic in her parent's inn. However, she knew the shadows were still out there.

'Can't you just wake up?' he asked, his hands shaking with fear. 'You don't want to know what'll happen if they find us. Wake up! Just get out of here, Kialessa!'

'I'm still trying!'

'Are you really?'

She was breathing so hard it was suffocating her. They tried pinching her, and then Kiel materialised water and threw it on her face.

'How do you keep making things out of nothing like that?' she asked.

'I just reach out like I expect them to be there, like when you reach for the salt on the dinner table without looking at it because you know it's already there. I just reach out for what I need, and there they are. You just reach …' He tried to show her.

She had no idea what he was going on about, and it didn't work for her. She just knew the shadows would find her at any moment, and in that very thought the shadows began to creep in.

'You'd better wake up soon,' Kiel said. 'You just gotta stop imagining how close they are.'

'Wait! What about safety? What if we just imagine safety?'

'I never thought of that,' he said. He ran around the room, materialising lanterns whose glowing flames helped to keep out the darkness.

'I like fire,' Kialessa said, trying to let it distract her.

A shadow's icy tendril suddenly touched her ankle, and she

leapt away as it melted back into the shadows. She knew, right away, that if they touched her eyes she would go blind, or if they touched her heart …

'I am safe,' she said. 'I am safe. I am safe. I am safe.'

Suddenly she forgot all about the darkness she was helping to dream and her mind filled with thoughts of safety. In the distance, she saw herself walking hand in hand with the king in a beautiful garden.

Yes, she thought, *that would make me safe.*

A second later she dreamed she was actually lying in her bed in the dormitory. It felt as if she was surrounded by a great white circle of The Eternal. She took a deep breath and the dream was suddenly over. She looked around at the room, still silent and peaceful in the night, with all the other girls sleeping in their beds. The night seemed so quiet. The dream about Kiel and the king's enemies a moment ago had seemed so real, now it felt strange and out of place.

It bothered her. Nightmares like this shouldn't keep waking her up when she had so much study to do in the morning!

By the next day she had forgotten the dream entirely.

 By Dr Joseph Ireland "Dr Joe"

The Fire

It doesn't take an extraordinary person to be a hero. It just takes an ordinary person, doing what's right, under extraordinary circumstances.

– King Dunnkan. Castle records. 85.1.313 CY

The next Myaday morning, all dreams forgotten, Kialessa thought it was the strangest thing; she saw someone she'd never expected to see again.

She and Piex were moving between classes when a curious looking trade caravan began to arrive. Three large, ornate wagons began to pull into the field next to the college. They were large, with 'Westfren's herb and medicinal supplies' written in large, friendly green letters on the side. Half a dozen men and woman, all armed, busied themselves steadying the posks and unloading the wagons. Then, leaping down from the lead driver's seat with superb confidence, was a human man. He was tall, but thin, and he had a slender, daring moustache that seemed to highlight the way his mouth seemed forever curled into a mischievous grin.

Kialessa gasped and hid herself behind the wall. With a stab of fear she saw it was the cruel, unkind man who'd held her upside down for everyone to laugh at last winter back at the inn. He was travelling as a guard with a spice caravan, and he looked as sly and cruel as ever.

She peeked out again, but she didn't think he saw her; he was too busy speaking to another guard.

Then she felt annoyed, *what was he doing here?* Was he here to cause trouble, or looking for more young people to torment? Whatever it was, she knew he'd be up to no good.

'What is it?' Piex asked, whispering beside her.

'It's him …'

'Who?'

'No time for that,' Kialessa cut him off. 'Have you any spells to turn me invisible yet?'

'Not yet.'

'Bother. Well, go to class then. I've a little something I need to do.'

'I'm not leaving you.'

'Fine,' she huffed. 'Stay here and keep watch. I need to get close enough to those spice guards to hear what they're saying.'

'Kialessa, you'll get into so much trouble again!' His breathing quickened.

'So go to class,' she smiled. She didn't want to miss this chance to find out what this man really was doing at King

By Dr Joseph Ireland "Dr Joe"

Dunnkan's castle.

Kia covered her horns with her hair and spiralled her tail into the small of her back. She took another way around; walked past the caravans and tried not to look out of place. She paused by the one the cruel man was next to, on the other side and, after taking a quick look around to make sure no one was watching, she dived underneath.

She pulled herself up onto the axle so that it would be harder to see her. She could hear his voice, but as they were outdoors it was hard to hear what he was saying at first. They mocked the ladies of the court and then discussed trading furs in the far woods. Then things got a little interesting.

'So,' the other man said, 'how long you been working as a spice guard?'

'New thing for me, actually,' the cruel man replied. It sounded to Kia as if a snide laugh lurked under his voice. 'Been hunting furs out in the western woods, if you catch my drift. Plenty to trade out there, been very profitable.'

The other man whistled and continued in a conspiratorial tone, 'Why'd you come back into the towns then, if trading fur's so great out on the western?'

'Who says I'm not still trading?' he said.

The other man was silent. 'Well, best of luck to you then. Better keep them furs away from the city guard.'

'Oh, I've a system,' the cruel man said. He sounded confident.

'So helping out a spice caravan is good for trade too?' the other man asked.

'Exactly,' he replied.

'Hey,' the other man suddenly whispered, 'did you hear?

There's another spice caravan down the road. Word is it'll be here in a day.'

'That's not good for trade,' the cruel man said. 'If the king finds out there's another caravan it'll increase competition for us. The duke will have to drop his prices till they're, I dunno, *reasonable!*'

They laughed.

It was all the information she needed. If she told the king, it would be one way to get back at him, and if they were overcharging for their spices anyway … As quiet as a feather she began pulling herself out from the axle when her whip caught on a pin and made a terrible scraping noise.

Kialessa caught her breath. If she was discovered she'd never get this information to the king.

But, as luck would have it, they didn't seem to hear her over their laughter. She slunk out from under the caravan and stood up, ready to run … and straight away walloped her head on the carriage step. 'Hey, what was that?' the cruel man shouted. 'Get down and look under the carriage.'

'I don't want to.'

'Go,' he ordered. His voice was threatening. The other man began to get down.

Quick as lightning, Kialessa jumped up onto the spokes of the wheel, too high up for him to see. She waited, not daring to breathe, until she heard him stand up again.

'Ah it's nothing, probably a bird. Forget it,' he said.

Kialessa crept away till she reached the steps where Piex was fidgeting, and then they ran to tell the king. They banged on the heavy throne room doors and a moment later the steward swung

     By Dr Joseph Ireland "Dr Joe"

them open and gave them a terrifying glare.

'Not you *again*!' he whispered in a bitter voice. 'If you're here to cause any trouble …'

'No, no!' she begged him. 'I need to tell the king something very important.'

'We're in important negotiations regarding some … unusually priced herbs.'

Kialessa and Piex spoke at the same time:

'That's what we're here to see you about!' Kialessa shouted.

'This is the very cause for which we are present!' Piex chorused.

The steward rolled his great eyes and bent his ear. She whispered her secret to him. His bushy eyebrows flowed upwards in disbelief.

'I will bring this information to the king. You go back to class,' he said in a dreamy tone, and, fingering his great emerald ring, he left.

Kialessa and Piex dragged their feet back to class. She hoped it had all been worth it because they had no real excuse for being late. They must have walked slowly for the news moved even faster than they did. They were just about back at class when a mean-looking person stormed out of a corridor and headed to the spice caravans. From the way the guards reacted he must have been the caravan leader. She hid behind a window to listen.

'Someone *told* them!' he roared. 'One of you bone headed thugs let out about the other caravan and now I'm pressing stones to get a single hundred out of the old boot!'

Kialessa smiled. It had worked!

The guards unloaded a few boxes at his command, while

Kialessa giggled to herself.

Then she looked out and gasped in surprise. There, looking right at her with a cunning smile, was the cruel man. He'd seen her.

She ducked back beside the window and was too nervous to do anything for a moment. Then she burst into giggles again.

'Serves him right,' she stated, and she and Piex skipped off to class.

***

It was lunch time when Kialessa received a little yellow note with the king's seal on it. Her four friends pressed around to see it as Piex read the message.

'Young Kialessa. King Dunnkan, honoured leader of the people of Lenmer'el, would like to thank you in person for the information you and your friends kindly brought to his attention. This has saved him and his castle a considerable amount of inconvenience. This kind of patriotic service is to be kindly rewarded. Sincerely, the steward.'

'No way,' Allastassia said in disbelief. 'You've been granted an audience with the king? In person! What did you *do*?'

Kialessa had to smile. After all, she'd already seen him twice before. 'Oh, I overheard the spice merchants plotting to overcharge the king for their spices. Piex and I told him.'

'Good going, Kia.' Darrix smiled, and patted her on the shoulder.

Posk immediately joined in, patting her affectionately on the back and saying, 'Good, good!' It almost knocked her over.

Kialessa smiled back at him. There was no way he could understand what she'd been 'good' about. It was just one of the six words he knew.

'I'm so happy for you!' Allastassia beamed. 'You'll have to buy a new dress, and have a wash. Really, you need a wash. Then we'll see the steward to make an appointment …'

'What?' Kialessa asked disbelieving. 'King Dunnkan? No way. I think I'll go see him right now.' And she stood up.

Allastassia tried to stop her.

'No, your hair, and your nails. You *can't* see the king like that!' Allastassia explained, voice straining to be patient.

'Yes, I can,' Kialessa replied. She had already seen him in far worse than the little blue and yellow dress he'd given her and she wore that every day.

'Kia, no, wait, you need to see the steward first,' Allastassia said, now trembling with concern.

Darrix laughed. 'Come on, Alli, it's just like her. Don't worry, I have a good feeling about this. Let's go with her.'

'But we weren't invited!' she said, now in a panic.

'It does say "you and your friends",' Piex explained. He seemed happy to wander along. 'What harm can be done?'

'Plenty!' she said, but she hurried to join up. 'You can offend him by being improperly dressed, or worse, you could offend his steward. Darrix! Piex! Oh!'

But everyone was already walking off, laughing. Allastassia ran to keep up, fussing about her hair the whole way even though she was the neatest of them all. Two moments later, just as they entered the inner keep and Kialessa flashed her little letter to the alert castle guards, she suddenly got the fright of her life.

There, walking in the opposite direction, was the greyhound.

She'd almost forgotten it. It was the same greyhound that had chased her up the tree.

She gasped and pressed herself against the wall, but it walked towards them, head down, as though it didn't have a care in the world.

'Hey boy,' Darrix said and patted it on the head. It nuzzled his hand in a sociable manner, and walked on as calm as the dawn, looking as if it belonged here, and walked this way every day.

'What is it, Kialessa?' Piex whispered to her.

'That dog …' she stammered. It walked past them.

'That dog,' she tried again, 'tried to kill me, at the end of winter, about twelve weeks ago, at my parents' home.'

'Whatever is it doing here?' Piex said.

'I … I don't want to know,' Kialessa replied. She clenched her fists to try and stop herself from shaking. 'That dog is magic. I know that. We'd better hurry.'

'Do you think it saw you?' Darrix asked.

'I know it did,' Kialessa replied.

'Whatever,' Allastassia said. She was not at all bothered by Kialessa's concerns about a dog.

Kialessa rushed them to the castle's inner doors, but instead of finding two vigilant stone statues, they found two statues silent as sleep. Instead of finding vigilant castle guards, they found nobody.

'Maybe they're all out?' Allastassia suggested.

'Not likely,' Darrix replied, the tension evident in his voice. 'The throne room is defended day and night, whether the king is there or not. It's not right for the posts to be abandoned.'

They all looked nervous.

Allastassia tried to hide her fears and moved to clean up Kialessa's face.

'This isn't right,' Kialessa said, as she avoided Allastassia and tried the door.

'Yes it is, you need to look your best … Hey, don't touch that door!' Allastassia complained, her enchantment fizzling between her fingers.

But the door was locked, barred from the other side.

'Now look what you did,' Allastassia whinged.

'I don't think the king is in,' Darrix said.

Kialessa knew something was wrong. She had the same feeling weeks ago, when the dogs first came for her, a terrible fear so deep down inside her she could hardly think. Then she smelt something odd, and bent her nose to the door.

'Wait!' Kialessa shouted. 'Do you smell *that*?' They all put their noses to the door.

It was *fire*.

'Get this door open now!' Kia screamed. The others just stood there.

'Allastassia, run and tell the guards! Darrix, find another way in. Posk, open this door!'

Then they ran. Posk looked up at the door with a curious expression, so Kialessa hit it and shook it and tried to get in. Then he understood. Rising on his back legs he whacked it with both fists, hard. The heavy oak doors rattled, but did not break.

Kialessa's eyes began to fill with tears. She screamed out for help. Her king was in trouble; she was sure of it. Oh, how could they get the door open?

The scent of fire was now clear. Posk looked at her and he seemed to understand the urgency. He took a few steps back, breathing deeper and deeper, his eyes becoming pools of black as some change she'd never seen before took place inside him.

Then, with a guttural roar a dragon would envy, he flung himself against the door with all his might. He split a fist-sized hole in the thick wood. Kialessa slipped her hand through the door and, with great effort, slid off the heavy iron bar that was holding it shut.

Honestly, you'd think they'd have better security ... she thought again.

The doors flung themselves open and a wave of heat rushed out. Kialessa heard all the windows in the throne room explode. The room beyond was a curtain of flames. The boys shouted out and fell back, but Kialessa just stood there. Her king was behind that fire.

Quick as lightning, Piex enveloped her with a magic spell, just like in training. 'Mage's momentum dampening body armour,' he explained. 'It won't protect you from the fire, but there may be complications inherent to this situation!'

Before he'd finished his sentence she rushed into the flames to find the king. She leapt through the entryway where the flames were consuming all the furniture. She pushed aside the choking smoke, trying not to breathe it in. It was difficult to see, but the smoke was much thinner inside.

Then she saw him. The king was lying face up in the middle of the throne room, a circle of fire creeping closer and closer to him. She could not see a single guard.

     By Dr Joseph Ireland "Dr Joe"

'King Dunnkan!' she screamed. She ran over to him. He moaned. Someone must have poisoned him. 'Wake up, we have to leave!' she shouted.

But he was too sick to move, and the fire was all around them. She searched his clothes. Surely a king held a miraculous healing brew somewhere?

The fire grew closer. It was too hot to be natural and seemed to be burning everything it touched, even the stone. Then, to her surprise and horror, part of it stood up and took the form of a giant dog, howling and glowing with blistering heat.

This was no ordinary fire. It was an elemental flame hound. It glowered at her with threatening jaws of flame, but there was nowhere to run this time. She stood between the raging, living fire and the wounded king.

'Get back, you fire!' she shouted in terror but, if fires could laugh, it did.

It took another step closer. As it moved, the circle of fire closed in on them. Kialessa then realised that there must be some kind of invisible protection around the king that it was trying to breach.

She jumped up and moved to push it away, but it gnashed at her without mercy. Its fangs glanced along the magical armour, and while it did not penetrate it the blow knocked her right onto her back.

She realised that if it got a good enough grip, it would crush her anyway.

The fire took another flowing step.

Kialessa looked at her bearded king. She trembled in fear and helplessness. She could not drag him through the flames, and the fire was going to be too fast for her to flee. But she could not watch him die.

Then her eyes fell on the golden hilt of his long sword. She heard his words echo in her mind: *You will do great things, for great good.* If ever there was a time for some great good, this was it!

With a shout she jumped up and pulled the golden blade from its sheath. A sword, how she hated swords! She turned again on the fire, and it pulled back just a little.

She heard Piex calling out something from down the hall. If only she could hold it off long enough for the guards to arrive!

The fire hound prepared to leap towards the king.

'Get back!' she roared and, stepping forwards, she swung the blade right across its face in a deadly swathe. The sword gashed against its jaw and almost twisted out of her trembling hands. It burst out with golden sparks.

With a cry of fear and surprise the flaming dog fell back and roared out in a strange language. It seemed to be telling her to get out of the way. But Kia did not move. She held the king's sword as tightly as she could. She knew she would give her life before she let the fire hurt her king. She felt a surge of determination, and a thin golden sparkle continued to dance defiantly along the blade of the magic sword.

'If you want my king, you'll have to go through me first!'

It crackled in derision.

'I am not afraid of you, **fire!!**'

She still trembled but was there was steel in her resolve.

Then she knew. It was not just the king she was protecting. It was everyone. If he died, the kingdom would soon die with him. She would not let this fire harm him!

    By Dr Joseph Ireland "Dr Joe"

9 For great good

Then the hound opened its mouth and breathed a torrent of searing flames at her, but this time it was Kialessa's turn to laugh. She was immune to fire, though it flicked all around her, covering her with dancing red and orange flames.

And Kialessa was small and very, very agile. She ducked under the flame hound's open jaws and then, with all her might, stabbed upwards and forwards with the golden blade. It felt as if she were pushing a stick into a sack of wheat.

The fire creature let out a tremendous roar and stumbled backwards, crackling and spitting in its strange language. Then, almost in slow motion, it fell backwards and dissolved into smoke. At the same time all the other fires in the room began to fade.

Kialessa heard the king cough and ran to his side.

'King Dunnkan!' she cried. She helped him remove a healing brew from the folds of his cloak and poured the strange blue liquid into his mouth, a process made all the more difficult by her sobbing; a mixture of her hidden fear and sudden relief.

'Kialessa!' the King then said in a slow voice, heavy with gratitude. 'I saw the whole thing. You risked your own life to save me! Thank you, thank you, thank you! A thousand thank yous will never be enough!'

She burst into tears again and hugged him as tight as she could. Of all the people she loved in the world, she could not lose her friend; the king.

'Kialessa look!' the king stuttered, 'your dress, it's all burnt to threads!'

'Oh, forgot about the dress!' Kialessa smiled through her thankful tears, 'you live, and that is what matters.'

By Dr Joseph Ireland "Dr Joe"

The Battle

You are good person. You were intended for great good. You have a body that is worth protecting. You have goals that are worth fighting for.

– From 'The year in jail', by the Tae'anaryn

In the next moment a half dozen fully armed and angry castle guards burst into the room. They nearly impaled Kialessa till the king vouched for her.

The steward rushed in next. 'My liege!' he said, almost in tears. 'How could I have let this happen?? I was tending the –'

'No apologies necessary, from any of you!' the king interrupted in a stern voice. 'This was obviously a well-planned attack. I'm all right now. We will discuss the details later. Where is the priestess?'

'She has been busy all morning with happenings in the town, and last I recall the wizard was called away not an hour ago on family duties. What happened to the guards at the door?'

'Dead,' Darrix reported in a grim voice, walking in with Kialessa's other friends, a bandage on Posk's hand. 'I found them in the next corridor. I think they've been poisoned.'

'This is a grim day!' the steward mourned.

'Indeed it is. Those were good soldiers, to be brought low by cowardly poison!' the King's voice shook in anger.

He sent others out to care for the bodies. Many soldiers were there now, while dozens more patrolled the castle. A pair of healers tended to the king, mending his wounds in seconds, and placing a new royal cloak on his shoulders.

Just then the priestess arrived. 'I had a feeling not an hour ago that you were in need, your highness, yet it seemed so muted, almost too easy to ignore,' she said. 'I regret that I was not able to pierce the shroud of evil that hid the danger to you.'

But the king was quick to forgive her, 'I cannot recall the last hour since the fire. How do you suppose someone was able to bypass the wards, and catch the guards unawares?'

'I … do not know,' she admitted, holding her head up though her lips paled in fear.

'I blame myself,' the steward mourned. 'Your Highness, how did you survive?'

'We have this young woman to thank,' the king said, resting a proud hand on Kialessa's shoulder. 'She arrived at just the right moment and fought off a creature of pure fire with my own sword while I was helpless and almost unconscious. She saved my life single handed!' He beamed.

'Yes …' the steward said, his trademark suspicion rising to the surface once more. 'How did you know how to arrive at just

 By Dr Joseph Ireland "Dr Joe"

the right moment?' he asked, probably hoping to find someone to blame more than himself.

Kialessa was nervous, but only for a second. 'You invited me. The letter?' she said, and the steward looked quite a bit embarrassed.

'That is … very good fortune,' he muttered, sighing with relief. 'It seems the gods are not yet done with you, my King, if they are so willing to intervene in your fate today. People *usually* make an appointment …'

Allastassia was here now, and thrust her hands on her hips in an "I told you so" kind of way. Kialessa had to smile, but precious time was wasting while the king chatted.

'What I want to know is who did this,' she said. 'Why did the elemental attack you? Was it the intruder, or does someone else want to harm you, King Dunnkan?'

In the next second there was a loud *crack*, whoosh, and the wizard, eyes burning with arcane fire and hands swinging a glowing staff, teleported right into the room, an impenetrable circle of lightning crackling all around him. Everyone leapt back in surprise.

For a moment he stood there, glaring at the room.

'I see you have mastered the situation already, my liege,' he said, disarming his fearsome defences.

'Yes, thank you,' the king replied, still clutching his chest in surprise. He sat back on his charred throne. 'And to think,' he smiled and said to Kialessa, 'I thought I brought you here to protect *you*!'

***

The king sat, while the people listened. 'You ask a good question, young Kialessa; who does wish to harm me, and the kingdom? There are many, many I have upset over the years, and others I have had to move from their lands to create public works …'

'You paid all fairly, and none seemed to me to hold murderous intentions, your highness.' The priestess pondered. 'Perhaps it was one who would benefit from your death? Your kindness provokes many criminals who are prevented from selling their evil in the kingdom.'

'The slavers?' the steward suggested.

'Perhaps … Kialessa,' the king turned to her, 'you are good at finding out things. What do you think?'

For a moment it seemed as if the steward would have mocked her, but he held his tongue when the king held up a hand for his silence. How she loved him, for King Dunnkan gave her words as much weight as anyone.

'You don't suppose it could have been the spice merchant?' she said. 'He seemed pretty upset when you found out about the other caravan.'

They all thought about this, and the king, priestess and steward all disagreed at the same moment.

'Not Duke Keesling,' the king said.

'Yes, and it seems an insufficient business loss to warrant such a reaction. Besides, what would he stand to profit?' the wizard said.

They thought some more. Then Kialessa remembered something; someone she still had a bit of a grudge for.

'I remember one of the spice guards,' she said. 'He's a cruel man who I've met before. He was talking about selling furs in town, and how the castle guards had better not find out.'

'There's nothing wrong with selling furs,' the king said.

'Wait!' the steward interrupted. 'Did he say where he got these furs?'

'The western forest, I think.' Kialessa replied. The room fell silent.

'No one hunts furs in the western forest,' the steward said. 'It is full of beasts of prey and bandits. They only trade in illegal things, like slaves and … poisons.'

'Search that spice caravan immediately!' the king shouted, standing to his full height. 'Bring me that spice guard!'

'Would that you had brought this information to us before, and not the arrival of the second spice caravan!' the steward said rudely.

***

Kialessa left the king and ran with the others, the captain joining them immediately. He led the charge, rushing down towards the caravans, when Kialessa drew up short.

There, watching them in total calm from just outside the main keep, was the greyhound. Its brown eyes watched them with human-like intelligence.

It was the eyes. Eyes she finally knew. Eyes she'd seen from being held upside down at her parents in last winter.

It was the cruel man. He *was* the Greyhound. So that was how he'd gotten to the throne room.

'There he is!' Kialessa screamed and ran at the greyhound.

'Child, where are you …!' the Priestess shouted.

But Kialessa drew her whip and charged on – she was not afraid of dogs anymore. She saw now that his plan was very clever. If the fire hadn't slain the king then they'd all rush down to search the spice caravan, and the King would be left with only a handful of guards in his throne room once more.

The cruel man *had* to be stopped.

For just a moment the dog looked surprised, then it growled at her.

'Get it!' Darrix shouted, 'It's the assassin! We're sure of it!'

Surprisingly, the adults took him at his word and began to charge after the dog as well.

The greyhound was very quick and in a few seconds had dashed all the way towards the inner wall. Just as it got towards the door a guard walked out and was knocked flat as the huge dog leapt over him with supernatural grace.

Kialessa tore after it, but the adults were so much faster, except for Posk.

Posk!

In less than a second she had him tethered and leapt onto his back, without even thinking he was on all fours and running faster than any of them. Up the stairs they ran, reaching the inner wall in moments and looking around.

But the greyhound was not on the left wall, it wasn't on the right. It wasn't even down on the ground.

'Where is it?' Kialessa shrieked.

'There!' Piex shouted from down below, jabbing his finger towards the roof.

The dog had somehow climbed right up the wall like it was the floor. She'd seen that before. Now it walked along a rope that was strung between the inner and outer walls; the ones that provided places to hang banners to honour the king.

'Help me up!' Kialessa screamed, and just like in training Posk gave her such a boost she almost flew up. With clutching hands she grabbed onto the wall. Using her tail to help hold on she scrambled up faster than she'd ever done before.

'Look out!' Allastassia screamed from down below.

The dog was almost halfway along by the time she put her first foot on the rope, it turned in shock, seeming almost surprised to see her. A second later the steward, the captain, the priestess, and half a dozen guards burst onto the wall. They levelled their loaded bows at the dog.

'Don't!' the steward shouted. 'You'll hit the child!'

'You won't get away with this!' Kialessa shouted, scurrying with confidence along the rope, whip now in hand, her tail helping her keep balance. 'You poisoned the guards and then summoned an elemental to kill the King!'

For a moment it just stared at them, seeming amused. It shook its head, like it was trying to get something off. Then the strangest thing happened, as though a grey coat was sliding from its shoulders. Its face moulded into a man's, and it stood up, a familiar grey cloak flowing from his shoulders.

It *was* the intruder! The greyhound was the cruel man, and the cruel man was the intruder!

They were all the same person!

He smiled. 'Ah, child,' he began. 'You really think my plan is as simple as that? This has taken years of planning, carefully itching away at the wards that protect the throne room. But you *had* to go stumbling in there and save him anyway. I should have never let you pass. I knew you'd be trouble, and now it seems once again that you are determined to interfere! Perhaps I should have killed you in the forest at winter's end.'

She paused… once again his voice sounded so familiar, she knew she'd heard it before. Like a bad dream she knew she'd had but couldn't even remember when she woke up… Like a dream …

Suddenly she gasped, as a thousand dreams flooded back into her memory. She finally recognised his voice – the smooth voice from her dreams.

'Your voice. Who's helping you!? Who are you plotting with to kill the king!?' she shouted.

This time he looked surprised.

'So clever … just like …' he muttered with a cruel, twisted grin as he balanced effortlessly on the rope, bouncing up and down on his heals gently as though he had all the time in the world.

He didn't answer her question. 'But I have my orders,' he said, the curved knife just appearing in his hand once more. 'And you just keep getting in my way …'

Suddenly he turned into sand, an instant later rematerialised in front of her, his curved knife pressed right up against her throat. Citizens held their breath, Allastassia screamed.

'Such a pity,' he whispered, only to Kialessa, 'but I'm not supposed to let you live any more, you know.'

Time seemed to pause. No one dared to move.

Kialessa struggled to breathe for the fear. She was about to die. She had no weapons, and nowhere to run. But then she remembered she had saved the King's life. If the cruel man killed her, they would find him, if not in this life, then the next. She held her head up and looked him in the eye, unafraid to die.

He laughed again, but his cruel jackal laugh cut short. 'So much … like your father …' he muttered.

Her eyes grew wide. 'What about my father?' she whispered, angry, no longer afraid.

Suddenly, without explanation, he put his dagger away. He stepped back till he was no longer in arm's reach, smiling as though he had nothing against her personally; this was all just … business, or a simple misunderstanding.

The others had taken up positions on both walls surrounding the thin rope.

'Surrender now, there is nowhere to run!' the steward shouted.

'Ah, ha! You'll not be taking me today Grudon!' the cruel man shouted in reply.

An instant later the captain let lose an arrow from his magical bow Hera Lira, and the cruel man only narrowly deflected it from piercing his heart. The wizard sent out three globes of pearlesque light, but the cruel man dodged them with impossible skill. He swayed on the rope, but did not fall. Then he laughed.

'Well done Bon Shur'e!' the intruder said in a compliment full of mockery to the captain. 'But I'm afraid I have no time to play today, not even with you, good high wizard Coeur DeFur. I really must be going. And high priestess Jacinthia, do give King Dunnkan my regards!'

He saluted them. Then he looked intently at Kialessa,

whispering so only she would hear it. 'You have *no idea* what is coming to your world, little tae'anaryn, and you're on the wrong team. *War* approaches …'

Before she could respond he did a perfect back flip on the tiny rope, and she almost fell off as it bounced around. She squealed and clutched on with both hands and tail; it was all she could do to prevent being thrown off.

He was like magic, leaping and twisting impossibly as he moved down the rope. They tried to shoot him, but everyone missed. Then the Captain redrew his bow, and time seemed to hold its breath, but the cruel man sliced the arrow out of thin air again, just the way he'd done with Kialessa's arrow. The Priestess commanded his body to freeze, but his mysterious powers shook off her divine command. The wizard conjured pure lightning into hands, but then held it as though it might burn the thin rope, which was all that was preventing Kialessa from falling to great harm as well.

She was edging herself back towards the keep, getting angrier and angrier at everyone's seeming inability to stop the cruel man. If he escaped, he would return. And if he returned, he might succeed …

Oh Eternal, she uttered the shortest prayer of her life.

Then she heard the steward swearing at the soldiers as well, pointing frantically with at the intruder and ordering everyone to take him out, the black rod clutched in his hand. Kialessa's attention was suddenly fixed on the rod of the king. She recalled that the rod held the promise of every person in the castle, maybe even the whole Kingdom, to protect the King. Murder was not in her heart, but while the intruder lived he could return and try again. There was magic in the world, magic in what people

    By Dr Joseph Ireland "Dr Joe"

believed in. Perhaps enough magic in the rod for a single wish on behalf of them all.

She twisted down from the rope and landed right at the steward's feet just as the cruel man leapt onto the outer wall. He kicked the fully armed guards and knocked them both out cold in a single move.

In the same moment Kialessa hauled the rod out of the steward's hands and he yelped in surprise. She turned the rod on the intruder just as he was about to leap over the walls.

'You will NEVER enter this castle again!' she shouted, and the sky shook with thunder, like a hundred thousand voices crying out against evil. Kialessa felt a torrent of energy swirling down at her feet, reaching deep into the castle, right to its roots, flowing to the very boarders of their land. The cruel man paused, just for a second, and it cost him. A bolt of white lightning exploded from the sky and struck him on his right cheek, scarring him. He fell clumsily to the ground against the castle wall.

'**That's** *Veridictus*,' the steward muttered, admiration evident in his voice.

'What?' she asked, the rod almost falling from her trembling fingers as it thrummed with power.

'A sacred sign,' the priestess said, loud enough for all to hear, 'a mark of truth. He must obey that command or suffer the consequences for the rest of his life.'

The cruel man touched his cheek, and looked out at Kialessa, murder in his eyes. Then a soft smile touched his lips and he suddenly turned into grey sand that drifted away on the wind just as a new volley of arrows pinned his grey cloak to the wall.

Kialessa screamed in frustration, he had escaped, escaped!

Her voice shot from her in a shrill scream that split the air and could be heard for leagues, a terrifying noise that might even scare away a cruel spirit forever.

***

Over the next few weeks they tore the kingdom apart trying to find *smooth voice*; the cruel man, but he was gone. At least he could never enter the castle again, well, not without setting off a painful *Veridictus* again, and not without the king knowing.

Kialessa knew it would be a long time before he dared to return anywhere to Lenmer'el. But when he did, trouble would come. Indeed, trouble would be what he sent even if he stayed away. War was coming, and the first harbinger of that war was the cruel man – the smooth voice, the intruder, the dog – who was plotting with someone powerful enough to destroy the King of Lenmer'el. Justice would have to wait, and Kialessa would wait willingly.

The Feast

If you've done evil, repent. If you've worked hard, rest.
If you've won a battle, celebrate!
– Dwarven proverb

Kialessa was laughing. The room was full of colour and dancing. Everyone was there at the feast the king held in her honour, including the king's three children and seven grandchildren. There were musicians and fire dancers, a great feast and a lot of music. All her best friends were there: Piex the wizard's apprentice, Darrix the prayerful warrior, Allastassia the enchantress, and Posk. No one knew what Posk was, but they all agreed he was the life of the party.

'Hey Kia!' Piex beamed. 'Look at what the king gave me.'

He shoved a big, heavy book into her arms. It was covered in dark mahogany leather and had an ostentatious display of Piex's family crest on the front.

'What is it?' she asked, although she already had a good idea.

'My very first spell book.' He beamed. 'Look, it already has several spells from each hall of magic, with space to write in many of my own! Oh, isn't it just beautiful?' He sat, clutching his literary treasure with delight. 'I'm going to scribe some illusions from the hall of Inflornum first. That's what I'm best at. Master tells me not to confuse shades with shadows, which really isn't the issue, however …'

It seemed as though Kialessa might be treated to another impromptu Piex lecture on wizardry when, suddenly, there was a bump on her shoulder.

'Apologies, Dame Kialessa!' Darrix teased her, using her new title in emphasis. The king had given her the title, which put her on the same footing as many of the nobles' children.

'Hey!' she protested, still at little unsure about a title that made her, technically, his superior.

Darrix watched her, a proud look on his face.

Kialessa wondered what he was trying to say. 'What?'

He nudged the dim silver shield he was holding.

'Oh. A shield. How nice!' she said. It was ornate, with a large decorative symbol of the Eternal on the front, scribed with sigils of devotion and faith.

'Nice?' Piex echoed. 'Kialessa, that's an alumium alloy. Forty per cent lighter than steel, yet just as strong.'

'It's still not as strong as the priestess' prayers over it!' Darrix boasted. 'Nor as strong as I will one day make it.'

'That's worth over a hundred gold pieces!' Piex protested. Then he thought for a moment. 'Oh, hang on, so is my book.

   By Dr Joseph Ireland "Dr Joe"

That's all right then.'

'All right?' Allastassia's voice rang out. They turned to see the young enchantress had joined them. A blue bird sprung from her hair and flitted out towards the windows. After all, it was early spring. 'What do you make of the value of my gift from the king then? I, who first raised the alarm?'

They bent down to see the large ruby ring on her finger.

'It doesn't appear to be magical, and there's no visible symbol of authority on it,' Piex said. 'What could it be for?'

She smiled. 'Not telling.' And, whisking around on her heels began to walk away.

'Her secret,' Darrix said and shrugged.

Suddenly Posk came racing past on all fours, sparks flying where two iron gloves with stylised lion heads clashed against the ground. Brushing past Allastassia he knocked her flat on her behind.

'Posk!' she squealed.

'Rmmmg!' he said. He turned to help her onto her feet, but then two flustered castle guards appeared. Posk gave a shriek of delight and ran away again.

'Posk! Don't leave me like this!' she protested, but he was away.

'What's with those gloves he's wearing?' Kialessa asked.

'Gauntlets,' Darrix corrected.

'And I noticed an enchantment to make them particularly effective against inanimate objects,' Piex said, without even looking up from his book.

Posk ran to the doors, but they were closed. He was cornered.

Kialessa knew what he'd do even before he did. 'Posk, don't

hurt the –'

There was a thunderous crash as the castle door was blasted aside by an overhead swing of the gauntlets. With a squeal of delight Posk ran out and headed for the forest.

'Fast learner.' Darrix smiled.

Allastassia joined them. 'Monster,' she muttered. 'Still, yes, congratulations Kialessa. I don't know what I would have done against an elemental flame hound. Then you tried to take on the assassin single handed! You're going to meet a lot of grateful people today. Don't forget to smile and say, "Nothing more than you would have done, I'm sure." Understand?'

Kialessa smiled. Dear Allastassia; still trying to give her a social makeover.

'So,' Allastassia smirked, 'what'd the king give you?'

Kialessa's mind flashed back to earlier that afternoon. If he'd been generous with her the first time they'd met, his kindness knew no bounds after she'd saved his life. He'd had her fitted out for three brand new dresses, including the beautiful formal gown for official celebrations she was wearing right now. He gave her a hundred gold coins and sent another hundred back to her mother and father, just to say thank you.

He had tried to move her sleeping quarters up to the palace, with a room of her own, but she'd refused. Instead, she purchased a simple duck-down mattress and a woollen blanket and stayed with all the other girls in the dormitory. It was her chance to live in privilege, but Kialessa knew it would make her lonely. Even noble children like Allastassia stayed in the dormitory. Only royal children got rooms of their own.

And yet the king had promised to treat her like royalty from

     By Dr Joseph Ireland "Dr Joe"

then on. She was instructed to be at all the feasts, and Kialessa couldn't wait to hear his stories and share hers every chance they had. He ordered every castle employee, from the washer woman to the steward himself, that if Kialessa wanted to see the king she was to be admitted without hesitation. His company was the best gift he could have given her. She was sure she'd see him often, probably at the end of the day after the far weightier concerns of running a kingdom were done for the evening, when he would enjoy her company the most. At least once a week, she promised herself, they would be seen walking the gardens in the evening, holding hands, talking about princes, palaces and all the lands beyond the mountains.

But her most expensive gift was supposed to remain a secret, and he'd given it to her before the feast had started. At the time they were in the newly refurbished throne room.

'Here!' he'd said to her, 'Pop off your college dress and put only this on!'

It was a simple burgundy sash, like the scarf, with three complex runes carefully sewn inside with glistening gold and ruby thread, and Kialessa was puzzled. But all the leaders in the kingdom were there: the wizard, the priestess, the captain and of course the steward, so perhaps there was something more to this gift?

She was eager to try it on, and as soon as she fit the sash her old clothes disappeared and the sash transformed itself into a beautiful night gown, as soft as lavender, magically warm like flannel, made of the purest silk.

It fit perfectly.

She spun around, and they all nodded and clapped their

approval. She twirled again. It was so comfortable she felt like curling up and going to sleep on the floor right away!

The wizard walked closer, looking serious.

'This is, needless to say, is an enchanted sash. Quite a work we did for this kingly favour, but it almost made itself! It *wanted* to be, Kialessa. You know these three runes there? They each reveal an outfit that is hidden magically inside, and at your command they will change.'

'Really?'

'Really. Your key words are; work: "*Operari*", college: "*Schola*", and rest: "*Requiem*". Obviously the night gown is for rest. The change is automatic and almost instantaneous once you deliberately and meaningfully say the key words. Try one.'

'*Schola*?' she tentatively asked.

And – *whippit!* – her night dress folded itself around and became a neat blue college shirt with a practical pair of skorts, perfect for both study and recreation. Unlike the first dress they'd ever put her in, this one fit, and was perfectly clean.

'Now anything you add to this outfit will become part of that outfit, and be hidden away when you change. It's a very useful feature, so use it wisely.'

Kialessa smiled. Now she knew the perfect place to hide all her belongings and they'd never leave her! No more placing of personal treasures in a silly old chest by the foot of her bed, with

By Dr Joseph Ireland "Dr Joe"

a lock so easy to pick she could almost stare it off! No more pretending she was carrying thick leather belt instead of a whip!

'*Operari*,' she said, without daring to look down. The king smiled.

Her college dress folded itself away to become the softest, strongest leather armour she'd ever touched. It fit itself tightly around her so that there were no pieces to be caught on carriage axles, and any swords or arrows would be hard pressed to cut open her magically enhanced second skin.

'Like all enchanted clothing, they are self-repairing and self-cleaning,' the captain said. 'Also, magic armour always resizes to fit its wearer, so it will grow with you.'

The steward continued, 'These are quality materials, Kialessa, far in excess of the current need. They will hold new enchantments very well.'

'But, best of all,' the priestess explained, 'your generous king had me work a little extra goodness into this armour.'

King Dunnkan smiled happily, a grateful little tear sneaking past his nose and concealing itself in his beard. 'That leather is immune to fire, as are you, Kialessa. No more will your outfit be burnt to threads while you're saving people's lives.' And he wiped a second tear from his eye.

It seemed the gentle king was almost always crying.

Kialessa ran up to him and gave him another hug.

'Thank you. Thank you all,' she said, but then she became serious again. There was something she wanted to know. 'What I don't understand is why the intruder, that cruel man, was trying to harm you. Is he really trying to start a war? I saw him, in a dream, plotting with someone powerful... I don't want harm to come you, King Dunnkan. Or to anyone!'

'A king has many enemies,' the steward explained.

'Especially those that would disrupt the people's peace!' the captain almost shouted. 'They would like his permission to sell them poisons, or make them into slaves. Or to start a war we don't need.'

'There's almost nothing more dangerous, or threatening, to the forces of evil in the world than a good leader, such as our king,' the priestess nodded in agreement.

'And there is nothing that stands in the way of harming a righteous king,' the wizard added, 'more than the people who love him.'

Kialessa was thoughtful. 'Then the love of the people can protect their king? I know. It was what gave the rod power to call down the *Veridictus*, wasn't it?'

The captain nodded, but the wizard looked concerned. 'It is true,' he said, 'but even so, there is no reason I can call on in either law or literature that can explain how you were able to do that, little Kialessa.'

'What do you mean?' she asked.

The steward interrupted to answer. 'The powers of the rod are many, yet there are none who may call on the *Veridictus* except the King, and his chosen protector.'

'And?' she asked.

'And' the captain explained, 'there can only be *one* protector. It is a sacred office, and that office is held by Honoured Lord Grudon Fletcherson, keeper of the rod, Lord Steward of Lenmer'el.'

The steward nodded soberly.

'A sign was given,' the priestess explained, 'a green star crossed the sky at the hour of his birth, the sign of the protector. Mya's certain witness that a new protector of the King is born. You too, were born under that sign, and I was privileged to foresee it. But in all of history only one has ever held that office at a time, so it is puzzling that you were able to do what you did before acquiring the formal office. There is no precedence for it.'

'Then what am I?' she asked. There was a pause.

'…We do not know,' the steward confessed.

'Ahh, this is all too serious for a young girl's celebration!' the King interrupted. 'The intruder is banished, and we are safe in this castle for a good, long time. Let us forget our worries and focus on the good that has been done! Come, ready yourselves for the feast!'

The others agreed and hastily prepared, but King Dunnkan stood, holding her hand, and smiled down at her.

'I hope you like my gift,' he said.

'I do!' She danced.

'That is very good. But Kialessa, I think it best if we try to keep this gift our little secret.' He gave a happy smile, and tapped his nose as if it was all a fun secret. 'Many feel you already generously rewarded with the title I've granted you. But I wanted you to have a proper outfit for when you need to … get to work.'

She smiled at her thoughtful king. 'You've taken a lot of

thought into what I might do for work, haven't you?'

He smiled, and knelt down to her height. 'What? Saving kings?' And they laughed.

King Dunnkan continued. 'You'll be whatever you choose to be, young Kialessa. I've noticed you listen to the council of others, but don't let them make your choices for you. It's one of the nice things about you, I think, and it's something anyone can do if they set their mind to it, but so few do. You have a lot more choices ahead of you, young girl. You'll need much more than good equipment, fine friends, and the occasional chance to be a hero. You'll need to know yourself. That is one of the most precious gifts of all and I cannot even give it to you! But I do know this one thing, Kialessa – you were intended to do great good in this world. Great good; you have a body that is worth protecting, and you have goals that are worth fighting for.'

She smiled, and off they went to celebrate.

***

Kialessa loved the celebration, and glowed with all the positive attention. But as the night aged and guests began to dwindle the late hours would find the young tae'anaryn girl curled up happily amidst the coals in the fire.

As she drifted off to a pleasant sleep she found herself wondering about how her life, like the seasons, had changed so much. Spring was finally here. She thought how this had all begun in winter when the cruel man had humiliated her at the inn, and how she'd begun to wonder if her life had a higher purpose. Now she had an answer, for a king had told her she was

  By Dr Joseph Ireland "Dr Joe"

not only to do great things, but great things for *great good*. Kialessa thought that was probably was true for everyone, but it was good to finally know that for herself.

With that thought she was satisfied.

Appendix

The Tournid Prophecy

The prophecy, earlier in this document, was written in Ancient on the Tournid stone, which was unearthed in the ruins of the fabled *Civita Aurea* in the 14th year of the Great Kingdom. No reliable interpretation is offered by scholars, most arguing in favour of the theory that it serves as a reminder of the confusion of war and the importance of moral vigilance, rather than as a prophecy per se. Also, while this translation (here provided by Academiclees in *The Ancients: Magic, Language and Literature*) is the standard it is still heavily criticised by others, notably Humdug, dwarf scholar.

     By Dr Joseph Ireland "Dr Joe"

Exalted Gods

Serros – god of the sun, keeper of laws

Lumos – goddess of the moon, keeper of times

Waglah – goddess of the waters, keeper of knowledge

Planas – god of plants, keeper of health and wealth

Annas – goddess of animals, keeper of love and family

Pumos – god of darkness, keeper of the dead

Mya – goddess of the earth, keeper of life

Days of the week

(Named after the gods of the heavenly thrones, or wandering stars)

Day name	Heavenly body
Myaday (start of the week)	The world
Lumday	The moon
Planasday (day of rest)	Brightest wandering star in the sky, always found near Serros
Serrosday (day of worship)	The sun
Annasday	A red wandering star
Waglahday	Second furthest wandering star
Pumosday (end of the week)	The wandering star furthest out, difficult to see by normal sight

Terms of address

In Lenmer'el and Emer'el. By Allastassia, 313CY.

Common Titles

Common folk. May only vote in local matters such as municipal law or mayoral votes, one vote per household.

Title	Description
Gentle	The general populace, such as in 'gentleman'. Someone who is not a 'gentle', such a scoundrel or thief, is not considered a person.
Honoured	The prefix 'honoured' can be used with any other title to indicate excelling respect or flattery. Commonly used with 'honoured gentle' to indicate a person of professional skill or accomplishment, such as a scribe or midwife.
Young	Title often given to children, indicative of future rank: such as 'young gentle' or 'young baron'.

Titles of Chivalry

Chivalry is the knightly class of the people, a rank above commoners. While they may only officially vote in municipal law, their words are often given weighting by the nobility class.

Title	Description
Sire or Dame	The lowest class of chivalry, a title born into or a title of honour bestowed by nobility or royalty for great deeds or accomplishments.
Sir, Madame	A higher class of chivalry, a title granted for many accomplishments, particularly mounted military. This is as

By Dr Joseph Ireland "Dr Joe"

high as most commoners can rise. Children are counted as gentles until they prove themselves. Also the proper title for royal advisers.

Baron/ Baroness

Highest class of chivalry. Title includes land (but not very much). Land typically passes to the oldest living child who is expected to care for siblings (and possibly parents). With new laws from King Duncan's father's time which allow purchasing land titles from others, a new class of citizens are rising to challenge the power of the nobles: the merchant barons.

Titles of Nobility

The nobility are the rich and powerful of the land, often related to the king but have no claim on the throne. They vote on all important civil matters such as taxation.

Title   Description

Count/ Duke/ Archduke, Countess/ Duke / Archduke,

The lowest classes of born nobility. Such titles must be gained by birth or, in rare cases, may be granted by the king.

Lord, Lady

A high noble (over many other nobles) or lesser royalty.

Honoured Lord/Lady

A noble deserving of extra respect, such as a church head or the high wizard. Other lords are supposed to defer to this honoured noble. As opposed to other kinds of 'honoured' people, this title can be granted officially, sometimes after a lord or lady retires or passes away. The title 'eminence' may also be used.

Titles of Royalty

Title   Description

Viceroy / Viceraine

First class of royalty, distant relative of king or queen, or proper title of the High King's closest advisors (and thus a promotion from nobility to royalty, however, children of such promotions receive no such honour unless they earn it themselves).

Prince, princess

Close relative of a king or queen. The title 'crown' is added if they are likely to assume the throne when they grow up (as in crown princess).

King or Queen

Sole rulers of a country, over many lords and ladies. Legal owner of all the land, granting land rights to subjects. The titles 'Majesty, Highness, Grace,' may also be used.

       By Dr Joseph Ireland "Dr Joe"

Points to Ponder

'The Tae'anaryn' is about fitting in at a new school, fitting in with new people, and finding your purpose in life. I hope it's a book that will challenge your thinking and have you asking questions!

This book asks a question, 'Is there a higher purpose to my life, and how will I know it?' This is known as an existential question: a question about existence and its purpose. Some philosophers feel there are no answers to this question, only the answer you give it yourself. Do you think there is a purpose to your life?

1. What was Kialessa's answer to this question? How did Kialessa go about answering this question? Who helped her answer her question?

2. Perhaps the most famous existential question is 'What is the meaning of life?', but this book only asks, 'Is there a purpose to my personal life.' Do you think your life itself has a purpose? How will you go about finding an answer to this question? What will you do if you don't find an answer?

3. What makes a life good? How will you know when you have lived a good life?

This book deals a lot with bullying.

1. Kialessa was trying to 'do the five'. Can you tell when she: 1. Spoke friendly 2. Spoke firmly 3. Ignored 4. Walked away 5. Reported.

2. Was there a time when she didn't deal with bullying appropriately?

3. How did she deal with having no friends at all at first?

4. How did she decide to deal with the 'annoying boy'?

5. What two reasons did Piex and Darrix give for bullying? Are these ever reasons some people might bully you?

6. How did she deal with Allastassia? How would you?

7. Is there a difference between bullying and teasing? Is teasing among friends all right? How do you let your friends know when their teasing is going a bit too far?

Quest of the Tae'anaryn

What bad thing happened to Kialessa at the inn? What would you do if this happened to you?

Even though a terrible thing happened, it made Kialessa begin to wonder about an important thing. What question did it make Kialessa ask?

The Threat

Who helped Kialessa escape the dog attack? Why do you think the dogs attacked her?

What did Kialessa do to protect herself during the dog attack, and afterwards?

The King's Guard

In this chapter, Kialessa gets a wonderful opportunity – to leave her family and live at an exclusive boarding college. What convinces her?

What would it take for you to follow your dreams?

 By Dr Joseph Ireland "Dr Joe"

Would you be prepared to go to boarding college? What would you be prepared to give up to follow your dreams?

The King's College

The college was different from the life Kialessa had known, but she insisted on having the experiences she believed she needed to grow. Do you think she needed to see the king? What would you have insisted on?

Right from the start, people (especially adults) had trouble with the way Kialessa looked. Have you ever been treated badly because of the way you looked or due to what you believed?

How do you think you should treat people in authority, who probably should know better, who treat you with unkindness or rudeness?

The King

What message did the king give Kialessa?

What do you think of the idea that people rarely rise higher than their expectation of themselves?

What influence can it have on a life if they believe they are a good person, intended to do great things?

The Wish

Should Kialessa have been out that late at night? Did she do the right thing once she knew there was an intruder about?

One lesson Kialessa felt she learnt was that: 'Good things come to those who wait, but nothing comes to those who don't wish'. What role do you think wishing and hoping play in helping us achieve our goals?

The Wizard's Apprentice

Did Kialessa do a good thing?

Is it all right to steal from people just to help a friend? Did Kialessa steal?

The Prayerful Warrior

Would you stand up for a stranger at college who was being bullied? What would it take for you to find the courage?

Do you pray? Does it sometimes surprise you who of your friends pray every day? How do you pray? Are there different ways different people pray?

The Chase

Kialessa's success in archery follows her belief that she can succeed. She pictures herself succeeding in the situations she wants before even trying. How important is picturing yourself succeeding? Does it help you succeed?

Would you chase an intruder through the forest? How much danger was Kialessa really in?

The Enchantress

Kialessa had a great success in this chapter, beating the college record. The tutor told Kialessa to: 'See everything in life as an opportunity'. Is it? Can even disasters turn out to be blessings one day?

Can the way we look, sound or our physical disabilities be what make us special or unique? Can they be opportunities?

What do you think of Allastassia's apology? Was it enough?

Do you think it's a good idea when apologising to someone for something you did to listen to how you made them feel, or is it enough to just say sorry?

The Half Troll

Posk is a mentally disabled student. Did he need special consideration to help him learn?

In what ways was he like everyone else?

Do you think Kialessa should be in charge of Posk?

The Senior Students

In this chapter, the five friends find themselves in an extremely dangerous situation with a real threat to their lives. What should you really do during a real bank robbery?

Do you think Kialessa and her friends were rewarded fairly? Why do you think the mayor was trying to keep their success quiet? What would you have done if you were the mayor?

The Dream Walker

Kiel, it turns out, has a special talent. Being able to control your dreams is called *lucid dreaming*. Have you ever had a dream where you realised you were dreaming and could control the dream?

Is it sometimes more effective, when chasing away bad dreams, to think of good things rather than try *not* to think of bad things?

Who do you think is trying to harm the King of Lenmer'el, and why?

The Fire

How did Kialessa know when to save the king? Have you ever had a 'good idea', or felt good about something, and it later turned out to be really important?

How did Kialessa find the courage to face such a terrible enemy?

The Battle

Who was the cruel man? What was he trying to do, and why? Will he be back?

The Feast

In the end, Kialessa was richly rewarded by the king. Why didn't she use the king's reward to live in the castle and become more privileged than most other citizens? What would you have done?

In the end, Kialessa felt she'd found an answer to the question of how she was to find her higher purpose in life. What was it?

Would her answer be enough for you? What do you think your purpose in life is? How can you go about finding it?

 By Dr Joseph Ireland "Dr Joe"

10 Baby Kialessa 'borrows' a cloak from a customer because she thinks it looks cute.

Kidnapped and tormented by an evil archmage who wants them to learn to harness the power of evil, Kialessa and Piex must find unexpected allies while they plan for their escape. It's not the wicked goblins, or the troll infested swamp, or even the towering rot dragon that keeps them there – but a simple riddle. Will Kialessa ever be able to return to her King and college again?

 By Dr Joseph Ireland "Dr Joe"

11 Am I evil?

Place the date and your personal mark here each time you read this book – libraries included!

Why not share your experiences and thoughts with the fandom! Get a grownup's permission and visit

www.DrJoe.id.au

for fan art, sequels, competitions and more!

 By Dr Joseph Ireland "Dr Joe"